SHADOW MOON

THE GODDESS CHRONICLES BOOK 4

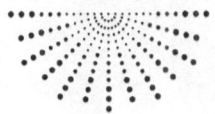

KB ANNE

Published by Gripping Tales, LLC, Pennsylvania.

ISBN: 978-1-956915-03-7

Cover Design by Anika Willmans, Ravenborn Covers

Editorial Services by Laura Parnum, Laura Parnum Books

❀ Created with Vellum

To Laura Parnum,
You get me!
Thanks for being an editor extraordinaire.
Any Ty9@s are my own.

PROLOGUE

The throne room was forbidden to Caer on this eve of Samhain, and she didn't understand why. As princess, she should have unrestricted movement throughout the castle, coming and going as she pleased just like she did at all times—well, with the exception of her nursemaid following her about, though Caer was talented at losing her. But alas, her father forbade her from entering it tonight.

She thought it cruel of her father and unforgiveable. She'd find another way in to watch the unexpected guests, especially on this most auspicious of nights.

Once, long ago, she had overheard her nursemaid talk about secret tunnels that wound their way behind the rooms and hallways of the castle. They led to underground dungeons full of monsters that would turn even the strongest of the guards to greasy pools of cowardice if not for the powerful magic cast upon them by her father's trusted Druid.

She had stalked around the castle, pressing on stones, hovering her hand over cracks in the mortar, and sometimes

1

kicking the impenetrable rock in hopes that she'd find her way to the secret tunnels. She'd had no intention of sneaking into the dungeons. Those monsters were best kept away from people. But the tunnels? Well, that was a temptation she couldn't resist.

She'd searched for the tunnels through most of the castle, patiently and painstakingly for many moons, until find them she did. The fates finally blessed her the night of Samhain. Earlier that afternoon her nursemaid had discovered Caer skulking around the castle in search of the tunnels and had punished the princess for her unsupervised wanderings by sending her to bed long before sunset. In a fit of anger and desperation, Caer sought to block the entrance to her room by shoving the dresser away from the long tapestry that had hung from her wall since birth. That was when she found the tunnel entrance at last.

Caer grabbed the torch off the wall and pushed the loose stone in. The creaking of wood pulleys and the grinding of stone against stone followed before the "door" appeared. Without a backward glance, she crept into the tunnel, shutting the door and her only known exit behind her.

She trod carefully along the musty passage, trying not to sneeze from the dust and mold. The bitter cold raised goosebumps on her arms. She wished she'd grabbed a shawl, but it was too late now. The Samhain ceremony would begin when the moon became visible in the night sky. She'd do without warmth if she wished to watch the festivities.

At each intersection, she closed her eyes and pictured the corridors that ran parallel to the tunnels. Based on her sense of direction she'd turn left or right, pacing off the length of the hallways she had traveled ever since her legs had been able to teeter down them. She wound her way through the castle, confident that she was heading in the right direction. But when she didn't arrive at the throne room when she thought she should, she began to doubt herself. Her father's castle was large, especially compared to the other castles she'd visited when she was younger, but still the throne room couldn't be much farther. If the tunnels went any deeper underground, she'd wind up discovering the dungeons, and she didn't have the stomach for real-life monsters. The ones in her imagination were enough.

When she was sure that Derg himself would open the gates to the Underworld for her, she heard footsteps thundering on stone. She knew her father had one guest in particular that he didn't want her to see—she suspected he was the main reason she wasn't allowed into the throne room that evening—but it sounded like hordes of guests were participating in the ceremony tonight. All the more reason to hurry.

A narrow shaft of light broke through from the stone wall and hit the opposite one. She listened first, priding herself on her patience and cautionary discretion. When it seemed that no one was standing on the other side of the peephole, she leaned toward it. She could barely see through the opening, but that didn't stop her from trying. Her father sat on his throne. In front of him stood the one she presumed was his honored guest. The one he didn't want Caer to meet.

He stood taller than any man she'd ever seen, including Percy and Roman, her father's most formidable personal guards. Her father smiled tightly at the guest—out of character for him. The King was known as a most hospitable host, and his reputation grew each time an enchanted bard came to visit. But this beast of a man was no bard. Even Percy and Roman seemed to shrink away from him.

"He must be deformed in some way," she whispered to herself. It was the only explanation for her father's cold greeting.

As if the man knew she was hiding on the other side of

3

the wall, he spun on his heel to face her. Gasping, she jumped away from her peephole. A large leather patch covered one of his eyes. She had heard of pirates that raided ships and raped and pillaged. The giant must be one. But why had her father invited him on the eve of one of their most sacred holidays, a day marking the beginning of the long winter, a day when the veil between the worlds was the thinnest?

She prayed silently to herself that he hadn't heard her, and if he had, that he wouldn't alert her father to her presence. Her heart raced. Her nerves were a knot of worry. She wanted desperately to watch the ceremony but was terrified that the giant pirate would inform her father that she'd snuck out of her room and was spying on them.

That's when the shouts began, soon followed by screaming. Samhain was a time of celebration and occasionally bawdy behavior with little cause for terror. She risked peeking into the throne room and soon wished she hadn't. The giant pirate brought a long, curved, jagged silver blade to her father's neck. Her father's eyes met hers, and he whispered something just as the blade sliced his throat.

Blood spurted from the wound, covering the giant pirate.

"No!" she screamed.

She watched paralyzed as the giant strode to the wall she stood behind. She managed to back away, but not before she heard him roar, "She's in the tunnels. Find the princess. She's my prize!"

"As you wish, my Lord Balor," his men shouted, and hundreds of heavy boots thundered out of the throne room.

Tears ran down her cheeks. She wanted to curl up in a ball and cry for her father, but not yet. Not if she wanted to live.

She couldn't return to her rooms. That would only lead to imprisonment, and she would not be a slave. Not to the giant pirate. Not to anyone.

As she ran from the throne room, her face pinched and her vision blurred, but it wasn't from tears. It was from something else. Something that felt an awful lot like magic. Had her father cast a spell on her as Balor slit his throat? She wanted to weep for the man who'd used his last breath to save her rather than to save himself. He was a noble faerie king, and she was nothing more than a spoiled princess who had snuck out of her chambers just so she wouldn't miss the festivities.

Soon her feet splashed in water. She must have reached one of drains that carried the castle wastes into the lake. How long before Balor's men descended upon her? Had they found other entries into the tunnels? Were they already searching the grounds? It was only a matter of time before she was caught, but she couldn't give up. She owed her father that much.

Her arms and legs ached with exertion—and something else. Her body seemed to be shrinking in on itself. But time was running out. She couldn't stop and figure out what was happening to her. Not with a giant pirate after her. She shook her head in anger. And to think she'd been worried about monsters in the dungeons—they were nothing compared to the one searching for her.

The water level rose until soon she was wading through it. It hindered her progress, but she refused to slow down. Goosebumps erupted across her skin followed by sharp pains, as if a thousand needles had suddenly punctured her flesh. She shrieked as she fought through the waist-high water.

Feathers poked out of her pores. She didn't understand what was happening.

Her arms and legs tucked up inside her body, shifting into wings and claws. An incredible pressure beat through her brain and exploded out of her nose—or what was once her nose. Now it seemed as if she had a beak.

"What's—" but before she could finish the thought, her body shot through the water like an arrow through the sky. No longer was she slowed by clumsy appendages like arms and legs. Now she swam through the water faster than she had ever moved before. She didn't know what her father had shifted her into, but she knew she was no longer completely human.

She dove out of the tunnel and plunged into the lake behind the castle. If she reached the surface too close to the castle walls, Balor might find her. She propelled herself through the water, pushing her new form to even greater speeds. When her lungs could no longer hold out, she broke the surface and took a deep breath. But it was no breath at all. It was a squawk, soon accompanied by other squawks. A cacophony of them. She found herself in the middle of a flock of . . . a flock of swans.

She'd never known a shapeshifter before. Had her father been one, or did he turn her into one to protect her?

A loud roar broke through the night. "Find her!" A man made that noise, but really not a man at all. Balor—part giant, part pirate, and part . . . something else. She didn't plan to stick around long enough to find out what.

A bright flash followed by a loud explosion erupted from the castle. Fire ignited the trees and brush that surrounded the castle walls, spreading across the countryside. Balor was going to burn down the world to find her.

And she refused to be his prisoner.

She was no longer the princess of the faerie king. She was Caer, orphaned shapeshifter who would be hunted to the end of the world. She didn't know where she would go, but she couldn't remain here.

Caer lifted her head, and her body followed. She flapped her wings and flew through the night sky. One hundred fifty swans followed behind her. They would protect her with their lives, just as her father had done.

QUEEN OF SWORDS

EARLIEST MEMORY

*T*he old woman found her curled up in the fetal position down at the water's edge. She didn't know where the girl had come from or what had happened to her. Only that she was covered with cuts, scratches, bruises, and dirt. The woman swaddled the unconscious girl in a blanket, making sure to blacken the white tufts of hair sticking out on either side of her head that marked her as being touched by the gods with their ancient magic. When satisfied that the girl's true identity was hidden from prying eyes, she tucked her into the cart pulled by her trusted pony, Nimblefoot, along with the shells, seaweed, and river rock she'd journeyed to the beach to collect. She took care to circumvent nearby villages and hamlets the girl could be from. It wasn't that she wanted to keep the girl for herself, but based on the condition of her young companion, something had happened to her that was not of the natural world. Her intuition told her that the girl was in serious danger and in need of her protection.

She traveled for many miles, climbing the steep mountains that led back to her hut. All the while the girl slept as if she hadn't slept for many years. The jostle of the cart, the bitter kiss of wind, even the harsh cackle of passersby didn't rouse the girl. At times the woman tried to wake her but to no avail. She feared the poor girl would die before she could tend to her with her own form of magic. When the woman was far enough away from prying eyes, she made a small fire and boiled a batch of nourishing soup for her passenger. The girl did not stir or open her eyes, but when the woman held up a spoon to her mouth, she swallowed the liquid.

After two days of being spoon-fed, the girl began to spend more hours awake than asleep.

"Where are you from?" the woman asked her.

When the child did not reply, she tried a different question. "What is your name?"

Again the girl didn't respond. The woman feared that perhaps the child was deaf and dumb, or perhaps the horrors of whatever she'd experienced had removed her ability to speak or respond to outside contact. The woman had witnessed such afflictions before. Sometimes, if the stars were aligned and if the proper herbs were in season, she could correct whatever damage had been wrought. But there were other times, times she didn't not like to think about, that the victim was lost. She hoped her young companion would be part of the group she saved.

Exhaustion wound its arms around the girl again and pulled her back into its embrace. A soft sigh, soon followed by a rumbling snore, told the woman her passenger would not provide much company for the next few hours. No matter. The going was treacherous, and it was best if she wasn't distracted.

Nimblefoot was proving to be well suited to his name. Even when he pulled the cart along the loosest scree on the steepest of slopes, he didn't miss a step. Energy pulsed through the air, hanging heavily in and around the cart. The woman wondered if perhaps the child was the source of it, but when she ran her fingers over her, searching for either an injury or magic, she felt nothing. She traced her hands along the edges of the child's face, thinking perhaps the magic was imbued in her. She murmured a searching spell as her palms hovered above the white feathers on either side of the child's temples, and there she found the source, deeply embedded. The most primordial power of love had been invoked to protect the child.

She gasped as a vision from the child's past came to her, marveling at what the poor girl had endured. Her passenger would be in great danger if ever discovered. It was more than happenstance that she'd found her. Destiny had played a role. Perhaps fate too.

Twice she heard wolves howling in the night, calling to their brethren in search of food. She had never feared the forest or the wolves before, but strange magic was afoot. She and the girl were in danger of becoming their next meal.

Nimblefoot snorted as if reading her thoughts.

"Of course you would make a tasty morsel too, but as you've always carried me where I need to go, I will ensure your safe passage through the mountains as well. Rather than dwelling on the virtue of our possible nutrition to the wilds, let's get on with our travels, shall we?"

He snorted again.

"Are you talking to your animal?" the girl asked. "And does he understand you?"

The woman smiled. The girl may be enhanced with ancient magic, but her questions suggested a bright heart and an eager mind. However, today would not begin their journey to Otherworldly discussions. Today, they would remain firmly in the world they were rooted in.

"It's good that you're awake again. I take it you're feeling better?"

"Yes," the girl said, stifling a yawn.

It wouldn't be long before the child found respite again, but if the woman could gather a few tasty morsels of her own about the child, she'd have much to ponder for the remainder of their travels.

"How is it that you came to the water's edge? Were you swimming?"

The woman often visited Lake of the Dragon Mouth to collect her seashells, seaweed, lake rock, and herbs. She believed them to be enchanted because of the mystical mist that hung heavy over most of the lake, giving observers the strongest premonitions that magical beings lived under the water and flew through the air, if not for their obscured vision from the mist. Aside from the profound magical elements of the lake, the waters would freeze even the warmest of hearts, the child being no exception. As the girl was covered with scratches, dirt, and mud, the woman didn't truly believe that her young companion had been swimming.

The girl clutched the blanket as if to ward off a chill. Or the truth. "I . . . I don't know."

The old woman flung another blanket over the girl. "No matter," she said, tapping her shoulder. "You may call me Mathair Mhór."

The girl drew the extra blanket to her chest. "Mathair Mhór? That is your name?"

The old woman blushed, remembering another child she had saved from a magical curse. A child who became a mighty warrior. Cu Chulainn, the great warrior of legends. "In a way. Someone once coined the name for me many years ago. It means 'great mother,' or mother of your mother."

The girl sat quietly as Nimblefoot pulled the cart across a wide brook. The sturdy pony knew the trail well. He also knew that in a few hours, his duty to his passengers would come to an end, and as a reward for serving them well, he'd enjoy a special mash of apples, carrots, and molasses over his oats and barley. He picked up the pace over the bumpy bottom, surefooted even on the most slippery of rocks. If one were watching, they might think the sturdy pony's hooves were magically enhanced, and they'd be correct in their assumption, but the sorcery didn't extend past the hooves. The speed was a product of Nimblefoot alone.

Water splashed their arms and sprinkled their faces as the pony trotted across the brook. Both the girl and the old woman looked at one another and laughed. Their eyes sparkled with excitement at the unexpected splashing they received.

"I would also like to call you Mathair Mhór," the girl said as they reached the opposite bank.

"I'd like that very much," the woman said, knowing that Nimblefoot had played a role in softening the girl's seemingly impenetrable surface.

"I am Caer," she said in a small voice. "But that's all I remember."

"And so it is enough." The woman smiled, and they began their final ascent to her hut.

Mathair Mhór put tremendous effort into keeping the white tufts of hair that framed the girl's face as black as the rest of her hair. She tried herbs and ointments. She even boiled liquid from nutshells and soaked Caer's hair in it, but charcoal was the only thing that kept it black. Caer never understood why Mathair Mhór worked so hard to hide her white hair or why she forbade her from swimming in the pond near their hut even to bathe, but Caer grew to love and trust the old woman and did her best to honor her wishes. She didn't remember anything about her life before the old woman had found her except for an immense feeling of loneliness that the old woman managed to fill.

Occasionally, Mathair Mhór left her on market days. She'd leave long before Caer woke up and make her way down to the village to trade her herbal concoctions for materials they weren't able to find in the woods around the hut. Items that other traders brought from far-off, exotic places.

Whenever she discovered the old woman wasn't in her bed, she'd wander the wilds around the hut, scouring the land in search of a broken fern bough, a snapped twig, or a soft impression of a footprint in the peat bogs south of their hut, but it was always as if Mathair Mhór disappeared with the morning fog and magically reappeared in evening.

Caer didn't know why Mathair Mhór wouldn't take her along. She seemed to like Caer well enough. She even called her *mo chuisle*, which meant "my pulse." Caer assumed that meant Mathair Mhór considered her precious to her, but every time she discovered the empty bed, she felt hollow and alone. She feared the old woman would leave her for good, though she never did. She'd always return with something sweet or a trinket Caer could play with in hopes that she'd be distracted from asking her once more why she had left without her.

As Caer neared her ninth year, and after begging for several moons, Mathair Mhór finally allowed her to go. It was a decision that would seal their fate.

The sights and smells of the crowded market with its unique foods overwhelmed the girl, but still, she couldn't get enough of them. This was why she had wanted to come. Soon, children of other traders pulled her into a game of hide-and-seek. They'd hide behind trees and rocks, and she'd find them and chase them.

Moisture beaded on their foreheads as they ran around the market. To escape the blazing sun, several children shed their clothes and dove into the refreshing pool of water formed by Danu herself as if she had carved the earth with her mighty hands, winding her way to the sea.

Caer stood at the water's edge. Mathair Mhór had insisted that unpurified water would eat away at the magic swelling inside of her. The only time Caer was allowed to bathe was inside the hut during the dark moon. Mathair Mhór would light the fire under the cauldron, then she'd help Caer clean the layers of grime from her body, saving her hair for last. Immediately after drying off, Mathair Mhór would reapply the charcoal to the white patches along with the strict warning never to bathe at any time other than the dark moon and never in front of anyone else.

But Mathair Mhór was too busy trading items to pay attention to what the children of the marketplace were doing. They laughed and splashed one another, continuing their game in the cool, sparkling water.

Caer dipped a toe into the pool. Mathair Mhór's warnings came rushing back to her.

"Come on! Come on!" the other children sang in unison.

"Are you afraid?" taunted a redheaded girl.

"I don't think she knows how to swim," teased the now-clean boy who had begun the game in the marketplace.

But Caer did know how to swim. She couldn't remember swimming before, but the water around her toe, and soon her foot, felt like a natural extension of her body. And she'd prove it to them.

She dove into the water and came up in the midst of them.

Once her head broke the surface, they shrieked, pointing at her as they backed away.

"*Bean sídhe*," screamed the redhead.

"Monster!" wailed another child.

"She's marked!" the boy shouted as the rest of them edged their way up the banks. Still pointing. Still screaming.

Hot tears fell down her cheeks where rivulets of fresh water once streamed. The white tufts of hair marked her as different, but she didn't know why.

That night Mathair Mhór gave her a ruby-encrusted sword along with a leather scabbard that could be slung across her back. Caer managed to choke out a thank-you for the generous gift, but Mathair Mhór would not accept her appreciation, claiming she was only returning what was rightfully hers.

Neither one spoke of either incident again. And they never returned to the village, even on market days.

THE LOVERS

*C*aer sat at the once rough-hewn table. She had spent many days rubbing the jagged edges with a piece of *slíogart* Mathair Mhór had gathered during one of her travels before Caer had come to live with her. It was Caer's eleventh year, and Mathair Mhór planned to pull her future card. The future scared Caer more than her past. Her past she didn't remember. It was as if she didn't exist before Mathair Mhór had found her at the water's edge. But her future caused her great concern.

Mathair Mhór studied her over the flame of a candle as she caressed the deck with the tips of her fingertips. "Ready?"

Caer pulled her lips in, giving a quick nod. It was the only reaction she would allow herself. Anymore, and she might change her mind.

She had witnessed the old woman pull hundreds of cards, but never had she taken so much time to build the energy in the room. As if Caer wasn't generating enough nervous energy for both of them.

Mathair Mhór's fingers danced through the cards with a

mind of their own, dipping and spinning in and out of them as she searched for Caer's future. All the while the old woman didn't break her stare with Caer. This should have filled Caer with calm because the old woman was so confident in pulling Caer's future, but it rattled her nerves into a tangled heap of chaotic emotions.

Mathair Mhór's eyes widened when she found the card. She withdrew it from the deck and flipped it picture side up on the table. "The Lovers."

The knot in Caer's throat dropped into her stomach. "What does it mean?"

Mathair Mhór's eyes glazed over as she fell into a trance. Caer should also have been used to this part of the reading, but it only solidified her fear.

"Your true love has returned to life on another plane. There he serves as a protector. The duality of his life will come to a crossroads. When he stands at the pinnacle of understanding himself, his power, and his true purpose, he will go on a quest."

She liked the idea of an adventure. It had been a long time since they'd taken a trip of their own. "What sort of quest?"

"He will go in search of you, though he won't know that purpose. He will fight for you."

Caer removed the sword from the leather scabbard behind her back and leapt up. The ruby-encrusted handle grounded her to this plane. "I don't need anyone to fight for me. I can fight for myself."

Mathair Mhór, unfazed by her outburst, replied, "It's not about what you can or can't do. It's more of what he is fighting for. He will find a reason to scour the realms to save you."

Caer ground her teeth as she glanced down at the card. She didn't like what she saw. "Why don't they have any clothes on?"

Mathair Mhór blinked, coming out of the trance. "They're lovers. They love each other in all their true forms. Their best attributes and their weakest aspects. They are the Original Lovers."

There was that knot again, but it erupted back in Caer's throat. She swallowed hard. "Lovers?"

Mathair Mhór nodded.

"When will this lover come for me?"

The old woman folded the cards back into themselves. "That is not for me to tell you."

Caer didn't like that answer either. "Should I expect him next week? Next month? Next year?"

The old woman smiled up at her, her eyes boring into Caer's third one—the point of energy on her forehead between her two seeing eyes. "When it is time."

"That's not an answer."

"It is for now."

Caer swung her sword in a wide arc, halting it at the tip of the candle. She didn't have much knowledge of using a blade but call it dramatic effect. "When?"

"When the moon aligns into the correct phase."

The candlelight reflected off the blade. "Which moon and when?"

"The answer is in the shadows, *mo chuisle*."

The blade hovered next to the flame. "When?"

"That is for you to discover."

Caer slashed the blade across the candle. The flame whooshed out as the sharp edge removed the wick. She returned the blade to its scabbard, angry and ashamed at her actions, and stormed outside.

It was the last time she and Mathair Mhór spoke on the subject of her future lover. It was the last time she and Mathair Mhór spoke at all.

. . .

Memories of Mathair Mhór and Nimblefoot were all she had now. That and a silver blade with a ruby-encrusted handle. Balor, the monster Mathair Mhór had warned her about, had burned down their hut in his mad search for Caer. Mathair Mhór and Nimblefoot were caught in the crosshairs of his rage and perished in the flames, innocent victims in his pursuit of her.

Caer honed the blade again along the stone's smooth surface. Someday she'd find Balor. She'd find him, and she'd stab him in the eye with her blade, thereby ending his life and his dogged determination to possess her at the same time. She owed Mathair Mhór and Nimblefoot that much.

It was soon after the fire that Caer found the portal. Mathair Mhór had spoken of a Shadow Realm, the Land of Shadows, where souls wishing to escape from the other realms' treacheries and chaos could hide. Gallean, a great wizard, resided there. The Land of Shadows dampened magic. It was why Caer sought it out. She had heard rumors that Balor retained a powerful sorcerer who could track Caer by a few strands of hair retrieved from the hut before it burnt to the ground. She'd been on the run ever since.

After Caer arrived in the Shadow Realm, she found that she could blend in with her surroundings and enter any place she desired undetected. It was the reason she was able to slip in and out of brothels and shops in the villages without getting caught. Bulging purses from a night's winnings were easy pickings if a person couldn't be seen. It was the reason she could pass through Gallean's three boundary spells without alerting him to her presence— others did not fare so well and often paid with their lives. And it was also the reason Gallean didn't know that she watched him as he trained in the arts of battle.

In the Shadow Realm Caer grew from a scared child to a

fierce warrior without ever even meeting her mentor, and one day she'd kill the monster who had taken Mathair Mhór and Nimblefoot from her.

THE HANGED MAN

*T*he clash of metal was unmistakable. Creeping closer seemed risky, but how else was she supposed to find out if this time the old wizard would be bested. It was doubtful, but still, she had to see. She'd watched enough of his battles to know that the bear could not be beaten by most men, but from the whelp of surprise that came from the keep, she suspected there was a woman present. Caer had never seen a woman battle the bear before. She had heard a rumor that if one could calm the beast, she would learn the secrets of everlasting life.

That was not a prize in her opinion. That was a curse. Caer lived with enough curses already. She had no interest in adding to her collection. Inevitably it would lead to her discovery, and she had come to enjoy this realm, or at least survive in it. She possessed no interest in searching for another one.

She pressed her hands against the cold rocks of the keep and peeked down the long corridor. The tunnel provided a decent view of the courtyard, albeit a narrow one. Some-times she scaled the walls and climbed in through a window on the second floor, but oftentimes the battle would end before she got there. It was better to watch without a full view than to miss it.

A long sword sliced through the air toward the bear. It was like nothing she'd ever seen before. She leaned closer. A narrow beam of sunlight reflected off the blade. It paused midair. For a split second, she saw the warrior—a man—and he saw her, or at least the shadow of her. The gentle spirit in his green eyes surprised her. He was under attack by the bear and fighting back, yet he demonstrated emotion most men, or at least the ones she'd encountered, weren't capable of feeling. He was like no warrior that had come before him. In truth, he was no warrior at all. He wore no armor. He bore no arms but for his sword. Because of that difference, she feared him the most. She should run away and hide from this potential new threat, but she couldn't find the strength to do so. She was a puddle of emotion—that also scared her.

The bear leapt at him. The hesitation from before vanished as the blade swept toward the wizard's heart. A gasp escaped her. She regretted it instantly and fell back against the wall to avoid being caught. Her heart galloped as fast as Nimblefoot's. She'd watched many battles and studied both the warriors' and the bear's movements. Never had she seen such practiced skill. She shouldn't risk it, but she scaled the wall and climbed through the window.

She had to know who this warrior/not warrior was.

The view of the courtyard from the second floor was much better than the tunnel but left her exposed, especially if the bear happened to look up and detect her shadow shimmying across the balcony. Warriors were typically too preoccupied with not dying to pay attention to their surroundings, but the bear—the bear was never very engaged in the battle. He toyed with the intruders like a fat cat might play with a scrawny house mouse right before swallowing it whole. Field mice might put up more of a fight, but the end result was often the same.

The man placed himself in front of a girl. "Girl" made her sound young. She was probably Caer's age, though age was not easy to access in this realm. The old wizard was proof of that.

The girl tried maneuvering out from behind him, but he appeared to be familiar with her tendencies. Without taking his eyes off the bear, he mirrored her movements to shield her. Her face pinched together, and she hissed in frustration. His green eyes sparkled with amusement, even as sweat beaded from his brow. Caer had not seen eyes as green as his. They reminded her of the green grass and vibrant plants of the Otherworld. Though she hadn't visited it through meditation since Mathair Mhór's passing, she'd never forget the vividness of that color.

The girl feinted to her left, then her right, and still the man blocked her. She was important to him—that much was obvious, but he was also a protector. It wouldn't matter what his connection was to her, he'd protect her, nonetheless. He was playful too—that's why he found amusement in blocking her, even while he was determined to either beat the bear or halt its progress. It seemed he didn't want to kill the bear, but he would if he had to. Caer sensed the conflict in him. It pained him to take a life, even that of an enemy. The kill would weigh heavily on him, and it wouldn't make the next kill hurt any less.

The bear lunged at him, temporarily consuming his attention. The girl took advantage of the situation—that was a strength of hers—and stepped in front of the man to face the bear without any weapon. She murmured something as she raised her hands, but nothing happened. Caer suspected she was trying to conjure magic, but magic wouldn't work in this realm. Many had tried, and many had failed. The girl was no different.

The man stepped in front of the girl as a breeze cut through the courtyard. Her hair moved with it. Caer stopped herself from gasping again. More than five years in hiding had taught her many lessons, one of them being, don't make the same mistake twice. Caer blinked to ensure she wasn't seeing things, but the black beneath the white was unmistakable. She reached for a tuft of her own hair and twirled it around her finger. The two were marked the same, but opposite.

She rolled onto her back and stared up at the sky. Mathair Mhór had once told her she was imbued with ancient magic, magic that was the product of a god. That was why Mathair Mhór worked so hard to hide Caer's white tufts. That was why Balor was after her.

For the first time, the battle ended peacefully for all parties involved. Of course the brother did receive a bite to the arm. Gallean didn't permanently maim him though. He bit him as a warning to demonstrate what the bear was capable of when provoked. And maybe Gallean wanted to test the man's inner fiber—weak and cowardly when attacked or ferocious and aggressive. The man's roar left no doubt.

Soon after the assault, the bear disappeared down the tunnel and the old wizard returned. It wasn't often that the wizard revealed his weaker form—though those who knew of the wizard knew there was nothing weak about him.

Caer tugged on a tuft of her stained white hair and tucked it behind her ear, though it always managed to pop out whenever she tried to hide it. As the visitors conversed with Gallean, she learned that they had traveled to his keep through a seomra de rúin and that their physical forms would return at the next Shadow Moon to train with him. Her mind was drawn once again to the man with the green eyes. His easy smile, his tall, strong body . . . he didn't resemble any of the village men. After quickly finding his key, which would enable him to leave the seomra de rúin, he chose to sit contentedly with the wizard while the girl stomped around the entire keep searching for hers. His eyes sparkled as he laughed with the wizard while the girl—his sister, Caer heard him say—searched everywhere for hers.

She watched from above for as long as she could until the girl approached the stairs to the second floor. Then Caer slid back into the shadows, slipped out the window, and climbed down the wall. She was reluctant to leave. It was the first time she'd watched anyone other than the wizard for longer than it took the bear to dispatch an intruder. The brother and sister were different too. Caer had spent many years with the sole companionship of Mathair Mhór, and now, she was alone. Her only company was the wizard who didn't even know of her existence. It gave her comfort that she would have three companions to watch train in the future.

A great sadness crept over her when the flash of light poured from the windows. She knew that the mysterious couple had returned to their realm and that she'd have to wait for the Shadow Moon for their return.

For restless nights after, Caer couldn't stop thinking about the girl and her hair and the man with the green eyes. She dreamt of him when she finally did sleep, and he was the first person she thought of when she woke up. She attributed her longing to her solitude, but a thought needled in her mind about the Shadow Moon.

4

A HOWLING TEA TIME

*T*onight we won.

Tonight Scott and I ensured a werewolf-not-shifting-and-trying-to-kill-me future. If we can hand out the nightlock-imbued crystals like party favors, and find Alaric and Lizzie, my future will be secure. And for the werewolves, the painful transitions from human to wolf to human can come to an end—at least for the ones wearing the crystals.

The Dark Moon ceremony was a success. The faint glow of the nightlock-imbued crystals in Scott's basket makes me smile. The spell worked. We actually conducted magic without destroying anything or killing anybody.

By the gods, we can be taught.

Of course, Scott's still afraid to touch them in the off chance that the spell can rub off, even though I've assured him a dozen times that the magic is inside the crystal—it isn't superficial magic. He can be such a dork sometimes.

On our way home from the Dark Moon ceremony, I sensed someone following us long before they revealed themselves. The signature of a werewolf is unique from all other humans, and though I don't know who it is, I know what it is.

"Friend or foe?" Scott whispers, clutching the crystal basket to his chest.

I cast out my mind in search of some indication that we either need to fight this stalker or ask him or her if they want to hang out. Of course, I hope it's Lizzie so I can convince her I'm not her enemy. Preferably by peaceful conversation, but if necessary, by force. My vines should hold a werewolf, and I've become quite gifted in growing them. As if to prove my point, one gently taps me on the shoulder. Okay, so I don't exactly have complete control over them yet.

"Well?" Scott whispers.

"Give me a minute."

"You've had two."

"Since when have you been so impatient?"

"Since gods have entered from the Otherworld, evil witches have tortured and tried to kill me, and now Lizzie has returned from the dead and Alaric and Breas are missing. Oh yeah, and there's the potential rise of the Fomorians and the release of Balor, some Medusa wannabe who needs four people to lift his eyelid because he would like to turn the entire world to stone. Yeah, I think that's the one that tipped the scales."

I roll my eyes. The effect is lost in the darkness, but at least I know I did it. "That's probably an exaggeration. I mean, how big can this guy be?"

"You saw *Harry Potter and the Order of the Phoenix*."

"You're basing your knowledge of giants on a work of fiction?"

"That's what you do half the time, and J. K. Rowling researched folklore."

I cradle the Chalice of Healing in my hands. I still can't believe it presented itself to me. "True, but there aren't many references in pop culture about Druids or Celtic mythology, so let's not make any assumptions. More of a wait-and-see approach. Or in the case of Balor, wait and not see."

"I prefer to be ready on all accounts. I don't like the idea of leaving this world unguarded while we train in the Shadow Realm."

"We've got time. Besides, a portal or a rip between the worlds can't occur until there's a full moon and the stars align in a certain celestial pattern and there's some major astrological event, and they all need to happen at once before nasty monsters can return from the Underworld."

"You also said that evil villains seem to know when that kind of stuff happens, and from your obscure memories of him, your husband seems like the evilest."

I punch Scott with my free hand while the other holds the Chalice of Healing. "Stop calling him my husband. It really makes me sick."

"But he is, or at least was. Are there divorces in Celtic god-dom?"

"I have no idea."

The signature of our follower fills my mind. "He's close."

Scott stiffens. "He? Could it be Alaric?"

The Chalice of Healing warms in my hands—or my hands are warming the Chalice of Healing, which may not be safe for the integrity of it—but Scott's mention of Alaric makes me lose my train of thought. I focus on the signature.

"No, it's not him." Sadness cools my palms, extinguishing the heat with it.

The werewolf is upon us now. Scott doesn't know that they'll blame me for the loss of their alpha. That they'll thirst for my blood for the sake of revenge.

I swallow my nerve and shout, "Show yourself!"

Madigan from Alaric's band walks out from the tree line.

"Madigan, what are you doing here?"

Scott tenses next to me. He's wondering if he can toss a crystal at him in case he turns.

He can't turn until the full moon.

Are you sure?

Scott, trust me.

"Gigi, have you seen Alaric?" If he had a tail, it would be between his legs.

"I haven't. Have you?"

His large trusting eyes study me before shifting away. "I haven't."

He's lying.

No duh.

"What's going on, Madigan?"

He's reluctant to share what he knows with us, but something makes him decide to. "There are rumors that you're responsible for Alaric's disappearance."

So my fears are warranted.

You're the Goddess of Prophecy. You often possess visions of the future.

And thank the gods Brigit decided to show up—and I mean that in the most sarcastic way possible.

Scott steps in front of me. "Why are they blaming my sister?"

Madigan shifts backward. He might be tall, but he's low on the chain of command. He's risking a lot by coming here —if it was his own decision.

"Madigan, this is Scott, my brother."

"I . . . I didn't know you had a brother."

"He just got into town. He was at the bar the other night. Remember, the drunk guy on stage?"

Madigan glances at him again. "I thought you were taller. You seemed huge the other night."

"Must have been the whiskey."

They evaluate each other. Well, it's more Scott deciding

that Madigan is most likely not a threat. Madigan already knows his place in their relationship.

"Madigan, who's blaming me?"

"Declan and his new girlfriend."

Hope blossoms within me. Could Lizzie be his girlfriend? I mean two werewolves howling at the moon together —why not?

"What's Declan's new girlfriend's name?"

"Maria."

"The girl from the bar?"

I knew she was a slut and untrustworthy, I plant in Scott's head.

I knew she was a slut too—that's why I wanted to hook up with her.

You're too good for her. Someday you'll find your swan.

In this body, feathers don't do it for me.

No, a large set of knockers do.

You said it, not me.

Madigan clears his throat as if he can tell we're having a silent conversation directly in front of him and he's politely waiting his turn. Scott and I really need to start restraining ourselves in front of other people. Neon signs shouting "God Here" would be less obvious. We both tilt our heads to encourage him to continue.

"I guess she wound up going home with him, and she never left. She's really intense."

The key to getting information from someone is to lull them into confidence. Madigan doesn't completely trust me, but he trusts Alaric. I might not be able to read his mind because of his werewolf nature, but I can tell by his guarded body language. "Would you like to come back with us and have some tea?"

"Tea?" Scott says.

By Madigan's expression I can tell he's surprised too.

"Yes, tea. We could stand out in the middle of the countryside in the cold, or we could get comfortable by the fire and drink some tea."

Do you think that's a good idea?

Alaric trusts him. He might know something.

"Okay, let's go get some 'tea.'" Scott thinks I'm going to drug Madigan. It's not a bad idea, but I'm pretty sure I can get what I need from him without it.

Madigan hesitates. "I don't know. It's late. I really should be getting back."

Scott lays his hand on Madigan's arm. "Come with us. Let's make it coffee with shots of Baileys in it. Actually, let's make it whiskey straight."

Madigan glances between the two of us. With Alaric missing he's unsure who to trust. Scott, sensing Madigan's indecision, gives him a look that would be difficult for anyone to refuse. It's a combination of "You will do as I say" intensity combined with Scott's natural charm with a little something extra.

"Yeah, sure. That sounds great."

See, no one wants tea in the middle of the night.

You compelled him.

What's a little compellation among friends? Do you think he knows anything?

That's why I invited him over. Plus, he seems lost.

So much for Maria.

You knew she was trouble.

Why do you think I asked her to dance? I needed some trouble.

She didn't have enough feathers.

You're never going to stop, are you.

Never.

.   .   .

Granda greets us when we get back to the cottage. "I've got a pot of water on. I thought we all could use a spot of tea."

"So much for the whiskey," Scott says in a low voice to Madigan.

He shrugs. "That's okay. I really just wanted tea anyway."

See?

Quiet, smart-ass.

How did Granda know we were coming? Does he have the gift of foresight like Clarissa?

"Children, you might be wondering how I knew you were bringing a friend in the wee hours of the night."

I glance over at Scott.

I thought he couldn't read minds.

He can't. He studies body language.

Scott slumps over. *What does this suggest?*

That I need to whack you over the head with a cast iron skillet.

He straightens back up.

Granda reaches out to shake Madigan's hand, and they exchange names. "I heard ya yammering all the way down the lane. Thanks be that all of Ireland didn't wake up with the lot of you wandering the countryside in the middle of the night."

Scott and I exchange raised eyebrows. Granda is yucking up the local Irish accent for Madigan, sounding more like a man at the pub than a scholar at the cathedral.

And it works. Madigan's shoulders instantly relax, and now that he's properly lulled, Granda abandons the vernacular niceties and gets to the crux of Madigan's visit. "I understand you're lost." He pours three mugs of tea and hands them to each of us.

"I wouldn't say I'm lost. I know how to get home from here."

Granda places the tips of his pointed fingers under his chin. "And where might home be?"

Madigan clears his throat and looks away.

"You've been to the meeting place underground, haven't you."

Madigan leans forward, preparing to stand. "I should leave."

Granda reaches over and grips his knee. "You don't need to go anywhere. You're safe here."

"I'm safe here," he repeats.

Is he compelling him?

I think so.

I didn't think non-god magic types could do that.

Granda is very skilled. We don't really know the extent of what he's capable of.

"Now tell me, Madigan. Why are you here?"

"Madigan's eyes glaze over. Maria sent me out to search for Gigi."

So he was lying to us. That's a shocker.

"Why?"

"She said she killed Alaric."

Tears spring to my eyes at the mere thought of Alaric dead and me having any hand in it. My entire body shudders with the effort of preventing a mental breakdown. Maria thinks I'm capable of killing Alaric? She didn't even know him before the other night.

"You may speak freely, Gigi. He'll not remember what you say."

I glance at Scott.

"Go ahead, Gigi. We have to trust Granda."

"What did you do, spell him?"

"I slipped him an honesty spell in his tea."

Scott pushes his mug away. "Did you spell me too? I thought we were over that."

"You and Gigi are drinking simple black tea."

I smell the mug, then smell Madigan's. I definitely can tell that something's been added to it. "Violets and cherry blossoms?"

Granda nods. "Well done."

I place my hand on Madigan's to establish a stronger connection. Between the tea and my own magic, we'll get some answers. "Madigan, why does Maria think I killed Alaric?"

His pupils grow to black discs, voiding the remaining blue of his irises. He reminds me of a demon, but I'm not afraid. He's completely under my power right now.

"The night Alaric went missing, she said she saw you at the Cathedral with him. It was the last time anyone saw Alaric."

"What else did she say?"

"She said that you were evil, and you had to be stopped."

"How did she find the pack?"

"Most of us live in a house on the outskirts of Kildare, close to Alaric. She showed up at our door the night he disappeared." As he finishes speaking, his face screws up in pain.

I rest both my hands on his so we're face to face. "You don't know how she found the house. Why? Is it spelled?"

He jerks his head up and down.

"And you let her in?"

He winces but forces the words out. "No, Declan did."

His body twitches like he stuck his hand in a socket. His arms and legs start to spasm as if what he's sharing is in direct conflict with someone else's wishes. Red blotches erupt across his face and neck, soon followed by red welts.

"Go on," Granda murmurs and begins a counter spell.

Scott's eyes widen in alarm. Maleficium is afoot.

"Why did Declan let her in?"

"She whispered something to him—I couldn't hear what

she said, but it made him kneel in front of her. She rested her hand on his head, then he rose and turned to us."

Whatever counter spell Granda cast seems to be working because the welts recede back into his skin. Madigan's no longer twisting in pain when he speaks.

"And what did he say?"

"He said that Alaric was dead and that you killed him."

The thought of Alaric dead gets me every freaking time. I swallow the lump before continuing.

"And you believed him?"

"Yes," he says in a small voice.

"Why?"

"Alaric was our alpha."

"Okay, but why would you automatically believe Declan?"

He blinks, his pupils still completely dilated. "Declan was Alaric's second in command."

"So that makes him . . ."

"Our new alpha."

"And what does that make Maria?"

"Our queen."

Madigan's eyes return to normal, the effects of the tea wearing off. "Whew, are you sure you didn't slip in some whiskey?" he says to Scott.

Scott winks at him. "Maybe I did. Why?"

"I feel a wee bit knackered."

I reach out and pat his hand to push out any remaining magic and ask him again, this time to find out how he'll answer on his own. "Have you heard anything about Alaric?"

"He's dead."

I clear my throat. I'll never find him if I can't get past the fucking concept that his pack thinks he's dead. He's not dead. I don't know where he is—Breas probably has him—but he's alive.

"Where's his body?"

Madigan scratches his chin as if he hadn't considered that part of the riddle. "I dunno."

Now to get him to admit truths without being spelled or compelled. "Your band thinks I killed him, don't they."

He glances away.

I grab his hand. "Do you?"

"Declan said you did. And Maria was the last person to see Alaric. She told us he was with you."

Maria again. What's her fucking deal?

"And what do you think?"

"That's why I'm here. To find out if you did it."

Deep down he wants to find Alaric. He doesn't trust Declan or Maria. "Do you think I'm capable of murdering him? I want to find him as much as you do—that's really why you're here, isn't it?"

"Yes," he finally decides. "I want to help you find him."

I smile. He gave us exactly what we wanted. At least now I have an idea who we're dealing with. "Madigan, would you do something for Alaric?"

He blinks, his pupils shifting back into discs. A little extra compellation motivation never hurt anyone. "Anything for our leader."

"Will you watch Declan and Maria and let us know what they're planning?"

"I know what they're planning."

"You do?" Scott says.

"They're planning to create an army of werewolves. They want to break the curse that binds the werewolf to the full moon."

"And how do they plan to do that?"

He blinks again, and his irises reappear. "They want to kill Gigi."

"Why?"

"She is the Goddess Brigit reincarnated. They say she killed our leader."

Scott hands me the empty teapot and gently pushes me away from Madigan so he can get close to him without being weird. "And what do you think?"

"I know that Alaric trusted her."

A thousand scenarios swirl through Scott's head before he settles on what he expects to be the best outcome.

"You trust her too."

"I do."

So Scott did some compelling of his own.

"You don't like being a werewolf, do you."

Madigan stiffens. "I didn't say anything about being a werewolf. Where'd ya get that notion from?"

Scott hands him a nightlock-imbued crystal. As soon as it touches his palm, the crystal glows.

"What sort of magic is this?" he whispers in complete awe of the power emanating from the crystal. My own crystal warms against my chest, reinforcing the power of any magically imbued yet naturally occurring object.

"That will keep you from shifting if you wear it around your neck."

He holds it up to the light. "Really?"

"Really," Scott says. "No more painful shifting every full moon."

He slips the leather thong over his head, letting the crystal rest on his neck. "Wow."

"Now," Granda says, appearing with a fresh pot of tea—I hadn't even noticed he'd disappeared— "let's get down to logistics and plans."

Madigan fingers the crystal again. "Let's."

WATCH OUT, DEVIL CHILD

*M*adigan left Granda's after we came up with a plan. Once he accepted the crystal, we didn't even need to compel him to do anything for us. He was more than willing to spy on Declan and Maria and report back to us when he learns anything. Scott worried about his safety because at the surface, Madigan seems, well . . . simple, but really he's just loyal to his true leader, and now that he knows Alaric is alive, he will do anything to assist his return. He wanted to go to Newgrange with us today, but we convinced him it would be better to hang around Declan and Maria, at least for today. But now I kinda wish he had come, because the conversation in the car is not exactly titillating.

Ever since our late-night visit to the fairy mound following our night of drinking and debauchery at Hell's Gate with Alaric and his band, Run with Silver, Scott's been quiet. Normally I wouldn't have a problem with him keeping his sidebar commentary about every random thought that enters his reincarnated god brain to himself, but I can tell something is bothering him. I mean, we had a lot of shit go down before the fairy mound incident and he still managed to talk incessantly the majority of the time, so the fact that he's not talking now is cause for concern. He didn t even laugh when I told him I was thinking about making black T-shirts that read "Team Alaric" with a giant white wolf on them for us and "Just Say No to Breas" shirts for Granda and Clarissa's coven since they've made it their life's mission to find the jackass god and the Vessel of Life—which I think is especially funny because now that Granda and Clarissa have realized they were spelled by Breas the night he came over to Granda's cottage, they are really pissed off. Evidently, it's acceptable for mortal humans (albeit Clarissa isn't exactly mortal) to spell reincarnated gods, but gods spelling humans is a big no-no. The coven's been canvasing the countryside, hitting every cottage and hovel from Kildare to the Irish Sea. Of course Scott and I have too, but our search, or at least my search, is less motivated by the Vessel of Life and Breas, and more by my desire to find Lizzie and Alaric.

Scott slips into an unusually long silence after my T-shirt joke. It makes me itch with even more concern.

"Penny for your thoughts," I say, smiling at him. My use of cliché ought to get some type of reaction from him. Dad rarely punished or corrected us, but when he did, it was always because of our cliché usage.

When Scott doesn't react, I think about swatting him, but he's driving. And on the wrong side of the car. And the road. In a foreign land. I probably shouldn't hit him.

"Hellooooo? Earth to Scott, Earth to Scott, this is your incredibly bitchy sister trying to get some attention."

Still nothing.

"Scott!"

He swerves into the other lane before swinging back into ours. Add shouting to the list of "What Not to Do While Driving in a Foreign Country."

"What the heck, Gigi? I could have killed someone."

I glance out the window at the countryside on either side of the road, then into the far distance. "You're right. Those *cáera* look like they plan to stampede."

"*Cáera?*"

I point at the herd in the far distance behind the wire fence. "Sheep."

He snorts. "Ms. Monacelli would never believe me if I told her how talented you are at acquiring a new language."

"To be clear, Irish isn't exactly a new language to either one of us. Well, some of the new slang is, but I'm not a complete fecking gobshite."

He snorts again. "I disagree. You are a complete fucking idiot."

"Hey!" I hit his arm and he swerves again.

"Feck," he shouts as he readjusts the wheel. "Careful."

"Sorry, you made me fecking angry."

"You're going to try and incorporate 'feck' into every sentence now, aren't you."

"Fecking right, I am."

He shakes his head, laughing.

"So Scott . . ." I start.

"So Gigi," he replies, and I'm reminded of the beginning of my conversation with Gram back in Vernal Falls following my cutting incident in school. Breas was the cause of it, or at least the tipping point, when he kissed Kensey right in front of me after kissing me the night before. I haven't cut myself since, but Breas brought out the worst parts of my nature. Now I know why. I think I'm stronger now, as I've mostly embraced my reincarnated goddess nature, but still, in a moment of weakness, I can't promise that it won't happen again.

But I don't want to talk about me or Breas. "You've been quiet recently. What's going on?"

"Don't you mean, 'You've been fecking quiet? What the feck is going on?'"

He does make a point. "Apologies for my fecking oversight, but really, what the feck is going on?"

He clears his throat. "Nothing."

"Something's bothering you. We've already established I'm not a fecking gobshite."

He laughs again. "I picture chocolate-covered raisins every time you say that."

"You're the fecking gobshite. Quit changing the subject. What the feck is going on?"

"Fine," he says, pulling into the Newgrange parking lot. "We'll talk on the way to the monument."

I don't want to wait, but obviously whatever he has to say is fecking huge, and he wants to give me his full attention. Of course, parking takes for-fecking-ever. The lot is mobbed with old people all wanting to get a look at Celtic history.

Should we wave our hands and tell them to look at us, because we're probably more ancient than Newgrange? I plant in Scott's head as I elbow my way past some senior citizens and wait for him in the grass.

That's exactly what we need—another spectacle made of us. "Get off the grass, miss," he says aloud, pointing to the small sign clearly stating, "Stay Off the Grass."

I roll my eyes and follow him down the path. "Why did Granda suggest coming here? I can't imagine Breas hanging around a crowded tourist trap with Alaric and Lizzie wrapped together with a fecking tidy bow."

"Maybe he wanted to get you off his case. You've been on him nonstop about finding them. It's downright annoying."

This time, instead of elbowing an old person out of the way, I shove it into his ribs. "What's annoying to me is that you're avoiding telling me what's bothering you, Mr. Keeps-to-Myself."

He sighs. "All right. Promise you won't laugh."

I stop in the middle of the path. "You know I can't promise that. There's usually too much fodder to just let it sit and rot."

"Right. I don't know what I was thinking," he says and hurries past me—definitely not the reaction I expected.

His hunched-over frame clues me in that I, once again, acted like an insensitive bitch. I rush to catch up to him. "Scott, wait."

When he doesn't, I yank his arm. "Scott, I'm sorry. I promise I won't laugh."

He looks down at me. The rims of his eyes are red. He's something of a softie when it comes to emotions. I never felt I could share those inner parts of myself, especially based on my fecked-up childhood (which turned out to be a lie, but the damage had already been done). But Scott has never resisted letting his emotions take him wherever they want to.

I pull him over to a bench. "What is it?"

He swallows hard. "Ever since Hell's Gate, I've had dreams of my true love."

"And this is a problem why?"

"It's getting to the point that I can't eat or sleep. I'm becoming obsessed with this image in my head. I don't know how much more of it I can take. I need to meet her or I'm going to lose it."

"Do you have any idea when that will be?" We leave for the Shadow Realm in less than two weeks. Meeting his true love before we go would certainly put a strain on the romance, not to mention affect his training with Gallean—and not in a good way.

"No, but she's all I can think about."

"Does she come to you as a human or a swan?" I try not to let my lip twitch. "I mean, whenever you lose your Oegden mind and sprout tornadoes, four birds circle your head when you get your shit together, and now a true love swan."

"Swan?" An old lady shuffles by. "Did you know that when two swans meet, they are bound together for all time? Their embrace inspired our heart shape," she says, tracing an imaginary heart in the air in case we don't know what a heart looks like.

"I have heard that," I answer for us both of us. "I've also heard that people shouldn't listen in on someone else's conversation."

Everyone can thank bitch Gigi for getting rid of the old broad.

She dips her head. "Forgive me."

"No, wait," Scott says and walks over to her. For the first time today, I let myself read his mind without his permission. He's about to confess who he is to this strange woman. He's always been far too trusting in my opinion, but it's not like him to share intimate knowledge about us. It's not just our lives at stake. According to Granda and Clarissa, it's everyone's.

"Scott, would you mind helping me with this?" I withdraw my never-ending spiral stone from my pocket. He glances at it, then at me.

Don't tell her, I think at him with all my power.

His mind drifts to the potential impact his "Confessions of a Swan Lover" could have.

"Forgive me," he says to the woman. "I should be going."

"Remember to be true to your heart," she whispers before continuing down the path to the shuttle bus area.

He returns over to me. "That was weird."

"Yeah, it was. We weren't even talking that loud. Do you think she's a spy for Breas?" I let my mind focus on the woman. She's still thinking about swans and true loves, and how true love shouldn't be kept apart. Nothing sinister or even mildly creepy, and no hint that Breas is responsible for her interrupting our conversation, but I'm skeptical. Breas wreaks havoc whenever he's around, and since he really is a god, I imagine he's capable of manipulating people from a distance to do his bidding. The real question is his range. How far away could he be?

I scan the area and notice some grass-capped mounds in the distance. It gives me an idea.

"Come on." I cut off the path.

"Gi, we're going to get in trouble."

I whisper an invisibility spell as I wiggle my fingers. "No, we won't. I cloaked us. Now come on."

But of course Scott doesn't completely trust me or my magic. He stops and pushes his arms out to the sides of the boundary. "I don't feel anything. I thought I'd be able to feel a cloak."

I roll my eyes. He's newer to the magic game than I am but, my god, he's so naive. "Do you think I borrowed Harry's invisibility cloak? I mean, seriously. A little faith here."

He crosses his arms. "If you can't prove we're cloaked, then I'm not going anywhere."

I release an exasperated sigh. "You were the one who was about to confess everything to the old lady, and now you want me to prove we're hidden? How am I supposed to do that?"

"Damien, come here!" a woman calls out. We turn to find out who this Damien is, because of course I'm picturing Damien from *The Omen* and wondering what type of magic I can project to stop a devil child from revealing us, or worse.

Scott, of course, is not thinking devil child possession. He's thinking child in danger. He squats down and holds out his arms. I'm guessing he thinks the child will run right into them.

Damien teeters off the path, veering toward Scott. I hold

my breath. It's the first actual test of my magic, and while I'm ninety-nine percent sure the cloaking spell will hold, that one percent is a real bitch sometimes.

The devil child approaches the boundary of the barrier at a fast hobble.

"Hey, buddy," Scott says. "Why don't you wait with me until your mom comes."

But Damien's crazed, sugar-rush-induced stare doesn't indicate that he's heard Scott or that he plans to stop any time in the near future. In fact, instead of slowing down he speeds up, running headfirst toward the cloaking perimeter and 3 . . . 2 . . . 1 . . . *Boing*!

Damien bops right off the boundary, shakes his head like poor Boo Bear—I miss that dog—and tries again. Then again. And unlike Boo Bear who can learn, and who better be well taken care of by Mrs. Paige, he keeps knocking into the boundary like he's the star of a two-second video on instant replay.

Damien's mother finally catches up to him and throws her arms around him before his next attempt.

"Mama, Mama, game, fun," he laughs, pointing at us.

She looks in our direction. I swallow.

"What game, sweetie?"

"There, there!" He points again.

Her forehead scrunches as she keeps staring. It's like one of those awkward encounters when the teacher pairs two students together who don't know each other and have nothing in common and they stare at each other in silence, wondering if they should say something first or let the other one do it while also thinking, "My god, why does she do this to me every time? Doesn't she know she should just pair me with Lizzie and be done with it?" Or at least that's what went on in my head when I was in elementary school, but you get the idea.

Thankfully, the mother picks up the devil child and carries him down the path. "There's nothing there, sweetie. Let's go see some big rocks."

"Rocks. Big!" Damien shouts, fist-pumping the air.

When they're far down the path, I finally release my breath. "Do you believe me now?"

Scott stares at his hands as he squeezes them. "That was weird."

"There's a whole lotta weirdness going on. After you're done praising me for my magic skill, we'll go look at those mounds. I think one of them might lead to Breas."

He rises, then bows before me. "You are a mighty wizard, dear Gigi."

Of course, only Scott and I and the rolling countryside are all that can hear his proclamation. Where's an audience when you need one?

"Finally, I get the praise I deserve. FYI, I prefer 'witch,' but 'wizard' will do. Now, let's talk fowl."

He follows alongside me. "Don't you always talk foul?"

I punch him in the ribs. "Not foul language. Fowl as in birds. Feathered creatures. Swans."

His mood suddenly turns solemn again. "Right, swans."

"So, before we were so rudely interrupted what seems like ages ago, what form does your Great Love take? Swan or human?"

I'm careful not to put "Great Love" in air quotes because, after the realization that Alaric and I have been together over many lifetimes, I will not judge anyone.

He sighs. "Promise not to laugh."

"I really hate when you put restrictions on me."

"Promise."

I throw my arms up. "Fine."

"She comes to me in spirit form."

Since I've had a variety of encounters with otherworldly

forms, and not just from the Otherworld, I need a little more information. "Go on."

He thinks about her, and I instantly see what he's talking about, but he needs to learn to use his words sometimes.

"Verbalize."

"She's not a swan. She's not a human. It's her essence."

"And her essence is making you sad?"

"You promised not to laugh."

"I'm not laughing. Merely asking."

"Did Alaric come to you in essence form?"

"No."

Scott picks up a rock and zings it at the nearest mound. "Shit. That settles it. I'm crazy."

"You're not crazy. Besides, I find that word offensive."

He picks up another rock and bounces it back and forth in his hands. "Then what do you call it?"

My initial thought involves a sarcastic comment about "fowl" minds, but I know that's not helpful, and Scott's really at a loss, so I decide to be completely honest with him for once.

"Alaric and I have been together in other lives."

"I thought you hadn't reincarnated since Saint Brigit way back in like 400 AD. And wasn't she celibate then because she was a nun? You are the opposite of celibate."

I knock him in his hip. "You're one to judge."

"But seriously, Gigi, when were you with Alaric in a previous incarnation?"

The flash of memory of Alaric and me together on a beach along the coast comes to me. Then another at a primitive hut with a small fire inside to keep us warm.

"A long time ago. Thousands of years maybe. I can't really tell when. I only sense pieces of us together," a lone tear streams down my cheek, "and apart."

He takes my hand and squeezes it. "We're going to find him this time."

More tears come, and I'm unable to stop them. "What if it's already too late?"

He cradles my face in his hands and stares at me. Warm fuzzy thoughts push out the sadness and fear that were once there. I don't know if he's compelling me to forget, casting a spell, or just being Scott with his firm optimism, but I guess it doesn't matter. "What does your heart tell you?"

I close my eyes and search for the truth. A small spark still beats there. "He's alive."

"Well, let's find him."

6

THE MAGICIAN

*C*aer studied Gallean's movements. Since the arrival of the brother and sister in the seomra de rúin, he'd been moving slower, more methodically. He'd stopped training with blades and swords and switched to using his own body. She watched as his hips swayed back and forth while he guided his open palms facing up into the air, gathering energy toward his head, then pushing it away from him as if in offering to his surroundings. Before the energy completely left his palms, he'd draw it back toward his body, flip his wrists, then lower the energy past his hips until his arms were fully extended and the energy was pushed back into the ground. She wouldn't call it magic, but she could see the energy moving with him as if engaged in an intimate dance between lovers.

This training seemed useless to her. She wanted him to use the blade. To make it an extension of his body and jab out at an enemy with the full force of his body and the weapon. She needed to learn how to slice off her enemy's head with a single swipe of her sword, without the weapon or her movement being hindered when blade met skin, then tendon, then bone.

Dancing with herself wasn't going to teach her survival skills if Balor's soldiers found her. She needed to learn how to eliminate his men, leaving no witnesses to inform him of her whereabouts.

Caer didn't know if Balor could penetrate the Land of Shadows, and she wasn't too keen on finding out. That's why she needed to stop the brother and sister from arriving. Sure, in the beginning she was excited at the prospect of watching the three train together, but if this energy dance Gallean had adopted following their departure demonstrated the type of instruction the brother and sister would receive, and by extension her, she wanted nothing to do with it. An energy dance would prove a useless battle strategy if she wished to remain alive.

She would take a portal to their realm on the morning of the Shadow Moon. She'd kill them and return without alerting anyone to her presence.

Even if Balor's sorcerer could track her into the Earthly Realm, they'd never reach her before she disappeared back into the Land of Shadows again.

"The problem with that plan, is that you'll eliminate the only two people who can help you," a low, gravelly voice said.

Caer blinked, her eyes refocusing on her surroundings. The wizard stood before her, reeking of sweat and scorn. She hadn't meant to lose herself in thought. It was further proof that the brother and sister needed to be eliminated. She'd spent years studying the wizard in secret, and now, in a lapse of judgment, she'd revealed herself to him.

"I've been aware of your presence since your first visit."

While she was shocked that he'd read her mind, she knew better than to reveal her emotions. He had taught her that much. She lifted her chin in defiance. "Easy to say now that you're standing in front of me. Maybe I just stumbled upon your keep."

He studied her. She felt his penetrating gaze as he took in her clothing, the sword strapped to her back that her fingers itched to reach, the blade hidden in her left boot, even the garrote she was slowly retracting from her wrist in a mad attempt to catch him off guard, wound him, and be gone before he alerted Balor of her whereabouts.

"In order to tell a lie, you must believe it. You stink of deception."

She gasped. "You're the one that stinks."

He threw back his head, fully exposing his neck, and laughed. She could shove the dagger into it and run before he knew what had killed him.

The rumble of his amusement echoed through the valley. "Had I known you were so entertaining, I'd have collected you sooner."

Collect? She would not become a part of anyone's collection. She reached for her sword, reacting on pure instinct. The wizard was the same as Balor and needed to be eliminated.

"Hold on," he said, removing her sword before she even realized he had moved. "I didn't teach you to sneak up on your enemies. That is the coward's way."

"So you are my enemy," she said through gritted teeth, hoping to dispatch him with the knife in her boot.

He swung her blade in his hand. "You will not wound me with your knife either."

"Get out of my head," she growled.

"But it is such an enjoyable place to be." He winked before turning around. "Come. We have much to discuss."

She watched the tall, hulking figure covered in animal skins walk away from her. If she leapt on his back, she could tug the garrote around his neck and be done with him before he knew what was happening. Then she'd leave and find a new place in the Land of Shadows to hide.

"I know exactly what you're thinking, and you will not succeed. You do not trust easily. Your flight instinct overrides your fight reflex, but I'm asking you to sit by my fire and share your tale with an old man."

"Why should I trust you?" she shouted at him.

He stopped and turned to her. "Because I know what you are."

"And what is that?" she spat. He couldn't possibly know her secret. She'd never heard of anyone else with her curse.

"It's only a curse if you allow it to be."

"Get out of my head," she growled again.

He offered his hand, his palm big enough to cover her entire face and squeeze the life out of her if he chose to.

"I haven't done that in years."

Hesitantly, she rested her hand in his. The smooth surface of his skin surprised her. For all his sword work, training, and wood chopping, she assumed his hands would be as rough and calloused as the rest of the wizard.

"You must first learn not to judge someone by their external appearance," he whispered, guiding her into the courtyard of his keep. He led her over to one of the wooden benches scattered around the fire pit before settling onto his own.

"Now, tell me, how is it you were able to penetrate the seomra de rúin?"

"I thought you could read my mind. You said you've been aware of my existence for a long time."

He folded his fingers together and pulled them to his chin as he studied her. "You were, perhaps, eleven when you first entered the perimeter."

She gasped. The stab of his betrayal brought tears to her eyes. She was so sure he had been unaware of her existence, that she could come and go as she pleased. "Why didn't you draw me out? Why didn't you take me in and care for me? I was a child."

He drew in a slow, deep breath. His eyes softened in the firelight. "You were a child. A damaged one at that."

His admission of the truth hurt. "Damaged? So you didn't want to care for me then? I was to be tossed out with your garbage if you took me in?"

"Caer, you were damaged, but not beyond repair. I sent a woman to care for you until you were ready for training."

"You sent Mathair Mhór?" Memories of the old woman she had come to think of as her grandmother brought a rush of warmth to her body. "Why?"

"The keep was no place for a young child. My angry bear nature doesn't just erupt when I shift into that form. I was not prepared to take on the care and training of a child. You've seen the visitors I've had through the years. I couldn't risk your exposure to my guests because even though they all take rigorous mental and physical acts to visit me, I ultimately do not trust anyone."

She rose to her feet. "So you're saying you sent me away to keep me safe?"

"I did."

"And when Balor's men lit fire to our hut and killed Mathair Mhór and Nimblefoot?"

"That was unintended and unforeseen."

"I thought you could see the future. I thought you were the most powerful wizard of all time."

His forehead bunched at the slight. "There are some things I cannot see. Mathair Mhór knew the risk. She was willing to take it."

"Do you think she wanted to be locked in her hut and burned alive?"

A fat tear slid down her cheek. She moved to swipe it

away, but not before Gallean reached it. It sat at the tip of his finger. He lifted it into the air before dropping it into the fire. As the flames kissed the tear, a vision appeared above them. A young girl covered in dirt and scratches curled up by the side of a lake. A bear watching from a distance as Mathair Mhór bent down to inspect the sleeping child. A magical aura covered them as she bundled the child and lifted her into her cart, while the bear lumbered off in the opposite direction.

"I thought you both were safe. I didn't think Balor's men could penetrate the magic I cast over you. Something about your energy signature makes you resistant to magic. At least my magic. I believe it's what allows you to enter my boundaries without notifying me of your presence."

"I thought you said that you knew I crossed your boundaries my very first day in the Land of Shadows." Accusation laced her every word.

His left cheek pulled in as he allowed a slow smile to play across his lips. "You were not as stealthy as you are now. I saw your head peek out from behind the wall before you learned to make yourself invisible."

"How did you know it was me? I was a young child the last time you saw me."

He traced the patch of hair next to her ear. Though the white was stained black to match the rest of her hair, the patches grew in tufts and stuck out no matter how much she tried to hide them. "You know why."

She knocked his hand away. His touch reminded her of a memory of her past, her father maybe, and she would not allow soft-hearted nostalgia to cloud her judgment. "So what now? Are you going to train me since I'm no longer a child and so breakable? Or are you going to train that stupid brother and sister in the art of dance that won't protect anyone?"

Gallean swept his hands into the air. A ball of energy swirled around him and he pushed it away from his body. Caer winced, thinking he was going to hit her with it. He drew it back into his body and pulled it up to his mouth. He watched her, his eyes twinkling. A wariness fell over her. She drew in a breath, knowing what was coming. He winked as he blew the energy ball at her.

It floated in the air. She watched it bop over, paralyzed to stop it. It hit her square in the nose and seeped into her skin. Her body absorbed the energy and reshifted it into something that might be usable to her in the future.

"Not sure how energy puffs can help in a fight," she growled.

Gallean smiled as he snapped his fingers, and then everything went black.

7

GODLY POWER . . . ACTIVATE!

A flash of lightning shoots across the sky. The air crackles with tension. I turn to Scott. "Did you feel that?"

He runs a hand through his hair, checking to make sure he's not rocking the finger-in-the-electric-socket look. "Feel it? I was almost hit by it! Where did it come from?"

I pat his shoulder to reassure him. "It must mean we're getting close."

"Close to what?"

"Wherever Breas is hiding."

Scott rubs his head again, not completely certain he wasn't hit by a rogue lightning bolt. Not that he thinks he'll find any dating prospects among the seventy-and-over crowd—he prefers females below the age of twenty-five—but he wants to be camera-ready in case his swan shows up. With his inability to control his magically produced tornadoes and the bird shit on his shoulder, his appearance should be the least of his worries, but I keep that sidebar to myself. Granda and Clarissa warned me that it was my responsibility to keep Scott in control of himself and to try not to agitate him. I made no promises, because I do enjoy agitating him, but for the sake of the surrounding buildings and, well, the world, I'll do my best to keep him calm.

"Is Breas the God of Thunder and Lightning? Because I feel like Granda and Clarissa should've shared that with us if he is."

"Scott, get over your man crush with Thor. Breas might be hot and muscular—I wish to the other gods that he wasn't —but he is no Marvel comic character who can call lightning to imbue his hammer with power."

Scott knocks into my shoulder. "I do not have a man crush on Thor."

I frown at him.

"Well, I mean, who doesn't, but what Thor does with his hammer is really no different than what you did with night-lock and those crystals."

I'd never thought about my magic like that, but he does make a point—not that I would tell him that. But still, some things are different. We are different. "I don't think my crystals will pack the same punch as Thor's hammer. And he's from Norse mythology not Celtic."

Scott considers my point while we walk toward the distant mounds. "In that case, Breas could be the God of Thunder."

It amazes me how much we both try to avoid our own godly nature. I don't know how much Scott remembers of Oegden. I only remember fragments that come to me when something or someone triggers a memory, but there are certain things we both just know, and we're far past ignoring it.

"Scott, we know Breas isn't the Celtic God of Thunder. Taranis is."

"Cut straight to the point, why don't you? I thought we

were going to live happily ever after in complete denial of our reincarnated god selves."

"If we could live in oblivion, I'd be all for it. Hell, I've spent most of my life striving for that state, but it's too late for that now."

"Talk about a reality buzzkill. I never thought I'd witness the day that Gigi Brennan embraced the truth rather than hide in denial."

I punch him in the arm. "Don't worry, I've retained my bitchiness."

He rubs it. "Oh good, at least most of you is still intact. But that still doesn't explain the thunder and lightning on a clear day in Ireland, which in and of itself is a rarity."

As if in answer, another flash of lightning strikes the ground in front of us followed by a loud growl of thunder. I open myself to the power generating in the air as a result of it. The old me would have called it some hippie-dippy shit, but this more-enlightened version of myself willingly allows herself to succumb to other channels.

"I think the thunder and lightning has more to do with the assembly of gods, both actual and reincarnated, along with the son of the Original Werewolf combining together to create an emergence of power. I remember reading about ley lines. Maybe Newgrange is on one?"

"Maybe," Scott replies before falling into contemplation. He's thinking about all the fecking shite we've been through —his shooting Ryan and how he wished Clayone had been the one that killed Ryan, or at least in place of Lizzie.

I drag my crystal necklace from Clarissa back and forth across my lips, wishing I could imbue Scott and everyone I care about with power that could keep bad stuff from ever happening to them, but unfortunately I don't have that power. If I did, I would have called on that shit back in Vernal Falls when Lizzie dropped through the floor of the church. My stomach flip-flops. A part of the old Lizzie, the part that was my friend—my best friend—has to be buried inside this new werewolf who thirsts for my blood.

Scott pinches my arm, abruptly yanking me back to Newgrange.

I rub the now-sore spot. "What the fuck? Was it necessary to jab your fingers into me as hard as you could to get my attention?"

"With all the wild stuff going on, I couldn't understand why you were ignoring me. I guess I sort of freaked out and might have," he pauses, a twinkle appearing in his eye, "overdone it." He glances around to make sure nosy swan lady, or anyone else, isn't eavesdropping on our conversation, but he needn't worry. We're still cloaked. "I also didn't want to risk doing any magic. You know I barely have control of it, especially when I'm anxious, and you ignoring me was definitely making me anxious."

A pain shoots down my elbow as I rub an especially sore spot. "Just remember you're an oversized ape and freakishly strong."

A grin appears as he flexes his muscles. "At least my well-tuned body is still my own."

I roll my eyes as we continue walking across the grass. "Lucky me."

He falls in step beside me, and the day returns to what appears to be another fruitless search for Breas, and by association Alaric and Lizzie. Or at least I think it does until my face, followed by my body, hits an impenetrable surface and knocks me backward.

"What in the gods?" I groan, rubbing my face, the last remnants of whatever I crashed into remaining.

"What the fuck?" Scott curses, and I realize he also got zapped. Evidently it hurt him more than me because he dropped the f-bomb, which only happens when he's teetering on the edge or really hurt. I don't need any excuse to use it.

I reach out with my pointer finger to see what will happen. The tip sizzles when it hits the barrier. I crabwalk away from the shock of it.

"Is it some sort of magic field?" Scott says, gingerly reaching his booted foot toward it. He jerks it back just before reaching the spot where I got zapped. "I can't do it."

"Chicken," I whisper under my breath. Not so that Scott doesn't hear me, but so whoever is the creator of such mumbo jumbo doesn't. When Hermione and Harry were on one side of their Shield Charm, they could hear and see the Snatchers. I didn't want to give anything away to Breas or whoever else might be behind this magic, or on the other side of it.

I open my palms and concentrate on the source of the barrier. "I can feel energy pulsing through it."

"Is it green energy or dark?"

I close my eyes and concentrate. "I can't tell. Only that it is really powerful."

"Do you think Breas is the cause of it?"

"He's the cause of all trouble, so yeah, I'd say so." Big deal if Breas heard me. He needs to know that it's never going to happen between us. And if he causes any harm to Lizzie and Alaric, he's done. Deep fecking shite.

"Gi, you can't let your emotions skew your judgment. Concentrate and tell me what you see," Scott says in the voice he reserves for small animals.

"Enough of the psychoanalysis bullshit. You got zapped too, and the only one I can think of who's powerful enough to create something like this is Breas. Carman too, but she's dead and buried."

Is she?

Great. Brigit has decided to make an appearance. *FYI, not*

really in the mood for you today. Unless, of course, you know where Alaric and Lizzie are.

You know I can't give you the answers.

How typical that goddess me would place restrictions on what she will share with reincarnated human me. It's like I automatically set myself up to fail as a reincarnated goddess. Typical.

I just want you to experience life. Remember what it's like to be human so you can better serve them when you return to the Otherworld.

If you don't shut up and let me think, it'll be sooner rather than later, and in all likelihood, it'll be in a body bag.

You wouldn't let that happen.

Want to try me?

Anger flames inside me. Brigit's testing me. I know that. But why did she have to be such a pain in the ass about it?

Because I know what you're capable of.

Chaos and destruction? Mayhem and bedlam?

No, you have the power to change the world.

Ah yes, the welfare of the world falls on me. Thanks again for that.

"Anytime you're ready to return to the world of the living . . ." Scott says. The annoyance in his voice further fuels my anger.

"It's not my fault that I have this thing living inside of me."

This thing has a name. And her name is Brigit.

"I know that you two have this love-hate relationship," Scott says, "but we need to figure out what this shield barrier thing is, and if we want to cross it or pass into it or whatever the feck we do with it. Or if we just walk away and pretend that none of this day happened. I am leaning toward the latter."

My annoyance at Brigit and Scott blossoms into a giant

fecking Venus flytrap. "If there's this magic shield thing it means we're on the very edge of discovering them. We can't abandon our search . . . now!"

He raises his hands. "Gigi, you need to calm down. Your anger will destroy you."

"You certainly aren't helping to stop it."

Magic swirls within me and around me. So does desperation. I have this feeling in the pit of my stomach that if we don't find Alaric and Lizzie soon, I'll lose them forever. In past lives, Alaric and I always found each other, then were ripped apart . . . over and over again, and that is bullshit. I don't want to wait another thousand years to be together again. What if we don't get another chance? What if this is it for both of us?

I want Alaric. Now. I want us to be together forever—and that might be foolish and naive, and maybe it's never going to happen, but thinking about that fucking bastard taking everything from me makes me want to break something. He killed Alaric many times over. He tricked us into releasing Clayone, and now Ryan and Dad are dead and Lizzie's a werewolf. He killed hundreds, maybe even thousands, trying to get the Vessel of Life from me. He may have even brought Balor into this realm in his wild belief that he could actually take over the entire world.

"Gigi, calm down," Scott says in a low murmur.

But it's too late. It's too fucking late for me to calm down. "I will not have Breas take everything from me!" I shout into the energy swirling around me.

"Gigi. No."

I ignore him. I'll use this energy, this magic, to find Alaric and Lizzie. I lift my hands into the air, balling up the energy around me. When it gathers to full capacity, I hurl it at the tourists.

The energy shoots through the air and covers the entire

crowd. Their eyes shift into blank stares and they turn toward us and march with one mind. My mind.

"What did you do?" Scott hisses beside me. "You have to stop this."

"I don't have to stop anything. I am the Goddess Brigit reincarnated, and it is time that I use my power, my abilities, my curse, to find Alaric and Lizzie.

"But, you saw what the shield did to us," he says in a small voice. "We're reincarnated gods. Magic courses through our veins, and still we were unable to penetrate the barrier without it burning us."

The crowd marches toward us.

"They'll be fine." I cross my arms and watch them. My magical energy was fed into the crowd. It would protect them. Wouldn't it? I shake off the doubt as they approach.

"It'll be fine," I say to Scott. "It will be fine."

"How do you know? How can you be sure?"

"I know." My answer comes out much weaker than I intended. "I know," I reply with more confidence this time.

The first of the crowd approaches the barrier. I suck in a breath. Scott's energy is swirling around him now, beginning to form his own tornado. I can't worry about him. He's got his own shit to work out. I need to find Alaric and Lizzie, and this is the best way I know how.

Scott's hands twirl in the air.

"No," I shout. "Stop."

But it's too late. Whatever Scott brewed up while I was distracted shoots through the air and hits the crowd. Our energies mingle together. Two young children approach the barrier. I swallow hard.

"I didn't expect young kids to be here," I say in a low undertone.

"You saw the same tourists I did. You saw families and the

senior citizens, and still you sent your energy without knowing what would happen when they hit the barrier."

"You're no better than I am. You sent energy at them too. What did yours tell them to do? Because it hasn't slowed them down or made them change direction. If anything, they've sped up."

Two boys and a girl hit the barrier at the same time, but instead of being thrown backward like Scott and I were, they immediately turn around and start running in the opposite direction. More soon follow, some hitting the barrier before turning around, others just following the rest of the crowd with our combined energy swirling above them.

We watch with morbid fascination as the entire crowd now runs away from the barrier toward a large pond.

"What are they doing?" Scott asks in alarm.

Before I can reply, three young men and an old woman wade into the water. The rest of them soon follow. The kids that led the pack toward the barrier are now ankle deep, then knee deep, then neck deep in water.

Why don't they stop?

"Stop," I scream, but they ignore me. They're making their way to the middle of the lake.

"Do something," Scott hisses as he takes off in their direction.

"What am I supposed to do?"

"You've got magic. Use it," he shouts over his shoulder.

If these people drown, it'll be my fault. I sent them into a magical frenzy. I commanded energy that I had no control over, and Scott added to it. I watch in horror as more and more people disappear under the water. I need to do something. I have to stop them.

I take a deep breath to ground myself. I gather the energy around me and this time I ask for Brigit's help. Tingles ripple through my body when she answers my request. We join as one, and a light, positive energy bursts through me and toward the water. It first hits Scott and a young boy he's trying to pull back to shore, but the kid's putting up a fight. As soon as the energy hits them, the boy stops. The dazed look disappears. The new magic worked. The energy spreads out across the water. Soon heads break the surface and I know that they'll all be okay.

"Thank you," I whisper.

Now you see what we're capable of. We're capable of beauty and giving life. But, if we use it with anger and frustration, we are capable of causing harm to the very ones we have vowed to protect.

I reach my hand out to touch the shield one more time just to see if it's there. My fingers crackle with electricity, but there's not the zap and sizzle from before.

Who is the source of this magic? Why are they trying to keep us out?

Maybe it's not that they want to keep you out, but they want to keep others in. While most of the portals throughout the world have disappeared, some still exist. And not all of them lead to the Otherworld.

What other places are there?

There are preserves for rare magical creatures on this world.

Unicorns and fairies. I can deal with them. Any glitter-farting ones?

There are also prisons. Similar to what your mother used to trap Clayone. Also what you used to trap him.

Dread turns my blood cold.

You mean there are more monsters out there? More monsters that me or somebody else could accidentally unleash?

When you feel powerful magic, you must be wary. Breas, while a god, does not command magic as well as you or Scott will once you've been trained. He possesses many limitations.

Can you just tell me where Alaric and Lizzie are?

I can tell you that they're not together, and they're not controlled by the same entity.

Does Breas have one of them?

And surprise, surprise—silence.

"I think that's enough searching for one day," Scott says, wringing out his shirt. "I'd say that's more than enough."

How do I tell him that there are magical preserves and prisons in this world? That there's more crap than we even thought?

Another day perhaps?

Yes, another day.

8

SIX OF PENTACLES REVERSED

$\mathcal{W}$hen Caer came to, she found herself tucked beneath a blanket but still sitting in front of the fire. She blinked a few times to clear the clouds of fuzziness still buzzing around in her head. It felt like the spiders that always appeared when the leaves began to fall had woven their way through her brain and she needed to strip away the webs before returning to herself. At last she shook her head to clear the final bits out.

"You were saying?" Gallean said to her. She could hear the laugh in his voice and refused to give him the satisfaction of believing he had gotten one over on her, which he most certainly had.

"Show me how to do that," she said, swinging her open palms up into the air to see if she could gather her own energy. She tried pushing out, pulling in, returning it to the ground, but she was incapable of conjuring anything except air. "Why is it that you can conjure energy and perform magic spells in the Land of Shadows when no one else can?"

He lifted another energy ball and blew it over to her. She

braced herself for the tingle and the blackout. This time it hit her stomach and she erupted into giggles. Yes, giggles. She couldn't believe it. The last time she had laughed with such abandon was when she had played hide-and-seek with the children down in the village. She shuddered as the memory of that day drove her laughter away as quickly as it had come.

"Stop messing with my emotions. And you didn't answer my question. Why is it that you can conduct magic in the Land of Shadows and no one else can?"

He drew his folded fingers to his face and rested his chin on the tips of them. "Gathering energy is not the same as magic. I cannot conduct magic in this realm."

She couldn't believe he was lying to her. He was capable of many things, but lying? She never would have suspected he'd stoop to that level.

"How do you explain the magic you've placed along your borders? And the seomra de rúin . . . isn't that magic? And why are the brother and sister coming if not to learn magic from you?"

"Did you learn magic from me?"

"No, but—"

"Then why do you believe they're coming here to learn magic?"

"Why else? You're Gallean, the most powerful wizard of them all, aren't you?"

"I didn't give myself that label. And though I will train them to use their magic, they will not be able to use it here."

"Then why are they coming? Why do you need to stop training with swords and knives and play around with energy balls instead?"

"Because an individual must learn to control and manipulate their own energies before they can manifest magic. By being in this realm, I've been able to pull inward and practice my other skills that were underdeveloped in the other realms. I overcompensated with magic rather than mastering my other strengths."

"And they are?"

He waved a lone finger in the air. "In due time, dear. And I did not create the seomra de rúin. Individuals from other realms who seek something from me do. All they need is a familiarity with my keep. But it needs to be an exact likeness or the seomra de rúin will collapse in on itself before the guest arrives."

"Why was I able to enter?"

"That is a question that will be answered another time. Now, we have much to accomplish before my other guests arrive."

Caer blew at the cold embers, hoping to spark life back into them. Normally, at this time of the evening, her cave would be warm and her belly would be full. Her unexpected day of training with Gallean had changed her in more ways than she fully understood. More ways than she would admit to herself. She shivered, tugging the fur tighter around her as she waited for the fire to catch. Gallean had offered her a room at his keep. Not a permanent living arrangement though, because she couldn't be seen once the brother and sister arrived, but a place for the period until then. When she had questioned him about their exact arrival, he'd waved off her inquiries as if he couldn't trouble himself with such rudimentary details.

Caer had considered taking him up on his offer. His company, albeit frightening when he was provoked, soothed her. But she needed solitude in order to mull over everything the old wizard had revealed to her. She couldn't fathom how he had known of her presence for years. She believed she could manipulate the space around her and disappear. And even when she was invisible, she was always careful not to make a sound when she watched his training sessions.

If he could see her, how many others could? All the inns and houses she'd snuck into to steal a loaf of bread or chunk of cheese while the people slept . . . She always figured the worst that could happen was, if someone woke up and they happened to walk into the room, they'd see nothing more than maybe a leg of lamb floating out the door—though most things she touched disappeared along with her. Now, she wasn't so sure. After all, magic couldn't be used in the Land of Shadows, and going invisible seemed an awful lot like magic. But when she disappeared, it never felt like she was conducting magic. She remembered what magic felt like when she had lived with Mathair Mhór and the old woman conjured a spell. Going invisible felt more like an extension of her, not something unnatural. She shuddered at the realization that if she hadn't been invisible all the times she entered a village, she ran the risk that someone might have informed Balor of her whereabouts. He had spies everywhere. Could he be on his way now?

She glanced around the cave. She had her sword and knife, a few logs, and a garrote. Should she leave and search for somewhere new to hide? Was there a place she could escape to where she'd be safe from him? She paced around the fire, jumping at every noise. She couldn't rid herself of the fear that Balor would find her.

Mathair Mhór had led her to believe that the Land of Shadows was safe. That it was the only place truly protected from Balor. The wizard wouldn't leave Caer exposed if she was in danger. He was powerful—that was why he could see the space between. That was how he had seen her.

To prove her theory, she pulled the space around her as

she always did when she disappeared and picked up a log. Indeed the log vanished along with the rest of her and didn't return until she placed it in the fire pit. Feeling reassured about her gift, she blew on the fire again. Red embers erupted, soon replaced by flame.

Her mind traveled back to another fire.

First the smoke had crept into her nostrils, waking her from a deep sleep on the rocky ground. She had leapt up, sword in hand, prepared to battle whatever intruder, be it beast or man, encroached upon her while she slept. She'd never intended to spend the night on the mountain after Mathair Mhór read her future card. She knew better than to leave herself exposed to the elements or an attack, but she was so angry with the Lovers card. How could a man save her? She was capable of taking care of herself. To prove it, she had stubbornly decided to stay out until the moon rose. But she must have fallen asleep. A soft breeze blew deadly promises, reminding her why she had awakened.

It was happening.

It had taken two years, but Balor had finally found her.

She'd never understood why Mathair Mhór forbade her from swimming or bathing in the open, but at that moment she knew. She was the reason Mathair Mhór's hut was burning. The laughter surrounding the innocent game of hide-and-seek had soon been replaced by screams as the children had run away from her in the water. Rumors of her appearance had spread across the land like the fire now consuming the place where she'd found sanctuary. The place she called home.

Sword drawn, she had sped down the mountain, but she'd been too late. Nothing remained of the hut or Mathair Mhór. Even Nimblefoot was gone. Balor had burned everything in his path to get to her, and he wouldn't stop hunting until he found his prey.

Caer pulled out her knife and dragged it across the stone, but mostly she stared at the flames, wondering if what Gallean had said was true. Were the brother and sister the only ones who could help her?

9

NOTHING TO SEE HERE

*T*hree days.

In three days Scott and I leave for the Shadow Realm.

In three days, at the peak of the Shadow Moon, Scott and I will take a portal and begin training with Gallean. If we don't find Alaric and Lizzie by then, I fear I will lose any chance of getting them back.

Three days is all I have left. It needs to be enough.

And who had been in the seomra de rúin with us? A movement out of the corner of my eye drew my attention away from Scott and the crazy-ass bear. That's when I saw her. And then the bear had let out an I-will-eat-you-and-like-it roar, and my focus shifted back to trying to stay alive and keeping Scott from becoming the main meal of Yogi's picnic basket.

I had forgotten all about her until now. Clarissa and Granda told me that only imagined objects will manifest themselves in a dreamscape. Other than Gallean, no other living thing can enter or exist in that space, or at least those are the basic rules. But I know better than anyone that rules are meant to be broken.

Will she pose a threat to us when we arrive in the Shadow Realm? I hope not. The fact that Scott and I can barely contain our magic in our own world when our emotions run wild makes me less than optimistic that we'll have any hope of accomplishing much of anything in the Shadow Realm. Throw in an unknown entity and I'm not particularly psyched about the idea of leaving our own world behind. Especially with Alaric and Lizzie still missing. But Scott believes that Gallean can help us. He's trying not to be selfish about it, but he's latched onto Clarissa and Granda's notion that Gallean will be our magical savior. Our only hope. Read: his last hope. He wants Gallean to help him.

And after the whole swimming-tourist incident, I guess I might need some help too.

Madigan climbs up the steep slope of the fairy mound to stand next to me. He stares off into the distance, the same direction I'm looking, but whereas I've disappeared into my own head, he's wondering what could possibly be captivating my attention. He's much easier to read now that we've spent a few days together. After several long minutes, he breaks the silence. "What are we looking at?"

I smile up at him. He adds a nice distraction from the stench of all the shite I tend to step in. "Sometimes I drift off into my head and think."

I don't know why I tell him this. I keep my innermost self shut off from most people. Even those closest to me I've lied to, but I've never even laced the truth with Madigan. I've always been open with him. He is the closest connection I have to Alaric, and that bond makes me want to tell him everything. To be open with him. When Madigan trusts someone, he will do anything for them, and now he trusts me —a concept that is fresh and new to me.

He pats my head like I'm his favorite pet. "Sometimes I

drift off too, but we've got to find Alaric, and from what I can see, he's not lounging on a stump waiting for us to find him."

"Right you are."

And I realize another reason why I like Madigan so much. He doesn't treat me like a goddess, even if it is just a reincarnated one. Scott, Clarissa, Granda, and all the other coven members treat me differently, even if they don't mean to. Scott, of course, is gifted in giving attitude back to me, but then in his next breath he cracks a goddess comment. Madigan knows I'm Brigit reincarnated—Declan and Maria told him—but he's not affected by it. I like that about him.

He rubs his hands together. "So, let's get to it."

Scott wanders over from the other side of the fairy mound. "Another tracking spell?" His tone rings with disapproval.

"Yes," I respond tightly.

Scott isn't in agreement with me about how much magic I'm sharing with Madigan, but he promised not to argue about it. Not to mention that a quick spell on my part ensured he can't bring it up with me ever again. It was one I remembered from the grimoire I'd found in Gram's attic. The very same grimoire that had briefly twisted Lizzie into an obsessed, psycho, dark-magic witch. After it had disappeared from the school attic following Lizzie's little exorcism on Kensey, I assumed that the grimoire was gone. But now, with the discovery of Breas's true nature and what he's capable of, I'm ninety-nine percent certain that he stole it along with Kensey. I don't care much about what he plans for Kensey—she was an empty-headed bobblehead in Vernal Falls with a diabolical need to make my life miserable—it's what he plans to use or has already used the grimoire for that concerns me. If I knew more about tracking spells, I could track the grimoire, and by default, Breas, and by accessory, Alaric, and by double added bonus, Lizzie.

Madigan hands me Alaric's shirt. It's the third article of clothing we've used to track him, and as of yet, we've been unsuccessful. I've also been unsuccessful in taking in a deep inhalation of Alaric's delicious scent before I use it for tracking. And not because it doesn't smell like him—I'm sure it does—but because of the judgy eyes of my brother and the becoming-familiar-but-not-quite-that-familiar eyes of Madigan.

"Scott, can I have the map?"

He rolls his eyes as he reaches into his back pocket and withdraws the folded piece of paper. "It's not going to work."

I grind my teeth. Ever since our field trip to Newgrange, our relationship has been strained. He thinks I went too far when I compelled the tourists, and even though it turned out okay in the end—mostly—he's been pissed about it and impatient to get to Gallean's. That disastrous day also reinforced Granda and Clarissa's belief that Gallean is the only one who can handle training us.

But still, a tracking spell is harmless. Except for the risk that Madigan might be caught sneaking into Alaric's cottage since Maria seems to have taken up residence there.

"Did anyone see you?" I fondle the shirt, trying not to imagine me ripping it off of Alaric.

Madigan slouches, shoving his hands in his pockets. My stomach knots. He looks guilty of something. I pray to the rest of the gods that he didn't get caught or reveal our plans to anyone from his pack. I've put a lot of faith in him based solely on Alaric. Alaric never actually mentioned anything about Madigan's trustworthiness, but my gut leads me to believe that Madigan is honest and dedicated to Alaric. Then again, my gut proved to be unreliable back in Vernal Falls before we knew that witches, werewolves, and magic existed. I've changed a lot since then. Hopefully my gut has too.

Shit, Scott thinks. *I told you we couldn't trust him.*

"Did somebody see you?"

Madigan's cheeks grow blotchy.

"Out with it, Maddie," I say, adopting Alaric's nickname for him. *Right the fuck now,* I mentally add, not wishing to offend either a sensitive soul or a downright backstabbing bastard whose ass I will kick before turning him over to Scott for another ass-kicking.

"Maria and Declan were otherwise engaged when I walked into Alaric's room."

My stomach rolls over but for a much different reason. "They were having sex in his bed?!"

He winces, backing away from me. I didn't mean to shout at him but, my gods, Alaric and I were never able to do anything in his bed. We were ripped apart far too many times. The one and only time I was in his bed was the night we first met at Hell's Gate. We were strangers. Well, at least he was a stranger to me—though he never did feel strange to me. I guess even then I recognized him from a past life or felt his familiar presence from Metropol in Pittsburgh or when he watched me at the football game or when he took me home after Breas almost killed me on the motorcycle . . . Whenever something bad happened, he was there to take care of me. And now, he's gone, and Declan and Maria are having sex in his bed.

"They're getting it on? Lucky them," says Scott, the guy who isn't looking to have a relationship with anybody. Although apparently he'd like a toss in Alaric's bed with Maria.

Madigan's face scrunches up. Clearly he's uncomfortable with sex talk. I applaud myself for not cursing at him—I probably would have made him cry.

"I wouldn't say they're having sex. It's more like she's taking from him and he's letting her."

"You mean she's blowing him?" Time to get out of the prude closet, Madigan.

His face turns beet red. It might actually explode. "No, I wouldn't say that either. It was more like he was lying on the bed naked, and she was straddling him, but her clothes were on. It was like she was taking energy from him."

Scott and I glance at each other. Madigan knows some things about magic, but he doesn't know everything. And he just unknowingly revealed that Maria must be one of Carman's pupils that Granda was worried about. Calliope and Carman might be gone, but evidently, she did train others.

Clarissa called Carman an energy vampire, I plant in Scott's mind.

What the feck is that?

Someone who drains energy from others to add to their own power and to keep them young and to give them power.

Scott shakes his head as if trying to rid himself of this supernatural magical nonsense that continues to settle around us. "What did they do when they saw you?"

I didn't think it was possible, but Madigan looks even more sheepish than before.

"Well, I . . . um . . ." he shoves his hands into his pockets.

I've never been a very patient person, but now, with Alaric and Lizzie missing, I am at the freaking end of my rope. And so is Scott.

"Out with it," Scott says. "Just get to it. What did they do when they saw you?"

"Well, you see . . ." he starts, then pauses.

I want to punch him in the face or kick him in the ass, but that's probably not the best way to get him to talk. So instead, and I'm quite proud of myself for thinking of this, I reach out my hand and touch his skin to my skin and think, *Tell us.*

"I . . . I can go into places, and people don't notice me."

Scott and I both look at each other and then him. We're both thinking the obvious. He's almost seven feet tall and weighs at least two hundred fifty pounds. There is nothing about him that could sneak into a room and not be noticed.

"Why can't they see you, Madigan?"

"So, you know that I'm a werewolf, right?"

We haven't talked about his werewolf nature since that night in Granda's cottage but I supposed we all came to a silent understanding, and now we try to put our complete faith in each other. Or at least Madigan and I do. Scott's surprisingly more skeptical.

"Go on," Scott encourages him.

"Well, before I became a werewolf, I was able to sneak into places without anybody noticing me."

"And how do you do that?"

"I pull the energy around me, and something shifts . . . and I'm able to go into places unseen."

"You mean to say that you can become invisible?" I mean, sure I'd love to have an invisibility cloak, but being able to do it on my own? I don't think so.

"Be nice, Gigi," Scott says. "If he says he can become invisible, then he can become invisible. I believe you, Madigan."

Leave it to Scott to take the diplomatic approach.

Invisible ass-kisser.

Just see what happens. I am not just a pretty face.

Madigan looks from me to Scott and back to me again. "I know you're having a hard time believing me. It's probably better if I show you."

"Yeah, you do that," I snap at him. It's not that I mean to take out my anger and frustration on Madigan, but to say that he can become invisible? Come on.

Madigan visibly takes a shaky breath. I feel like it's important to point out that it was a visible breath.

"I've never done it with anyone watching before."

Scott rests his hand on his shoulder. "Do you want us to turn around?"

Quit babying him.

Listen, if he can become invisible, do you know how much of an asset he could be?

He's got a point there.

"Sure, Madigan. We'll turn around."

And Scott and I turn our backs. I roll my eyes. I still can't believe I'm indulging this giant, but whatever. If Scott says he could be useful, I'll do it.

"You can turn around now," Madigan says.

We do, and he's ... he's ... gone.

10

TWO OF CUPS

he pain of an empty stomach didn't subside as she slept, but that was not what woke Caer. Balor came to her. The giant pirate man with the eye patch often haunted her dreams, but last night she remembered something of the time before Mathair Mhór had found her curled up along the shoreline of Lake of the Dragon Mouth. She remembered Balor staring at her through the tiny crack in the wall just before he sliced a man's throat. But it was not just any man's throat. It was her father's. For years she'd buried the horrors of that night inside the deepest recesses of her memories, but her day spent in the company of Gallean —after years of solitude—stirred emotions in her that tore the hinges off the locked door. And now that it was open, she didn't know what would escape.

With her heart trying to beat a hole out of her chest, she fell back into a fitful sleep. This time Balor wrapped a mighty hand around her throat and squeezed the life out of her.

Hours later, the ghost of his hand still clung to her neck.

She paused to steady her breath as she crossed the first border to the keep. It would not do well to worry about a past she barely remembered. Survival was all she knew, and soon she'd learn the means with which to kill the monster and end his hunt of her.

The pheasant swung back and forth from her hip. She'd found it this morning in the snare she had set the day before. She didn't know if Gallean's bear nature dictated an appetite for berries and fruit rather than fresh-caught game, but she brought it as tribute.

Caer still found it beyond comprehension that the wizard had sent Mathair Mhór to her. Tears welled in her eyes. She loved that old woman and still mourned her passing. It annoyed her that Gallean had waited until thoughts of killing the brother and sister stirred within her to reveal that he knew of her existence. He did seem ready to train her though. She would take that as positive sign.

As Caer passed through the third and final barrier, Gallean stood at the entrance to his keep.

"Thank you for bringing breakfast," he said, removing the pheasant from her belt. She was relieved that her concerns about him not eating meat were unwarranted.

The sight of the wizard calmed her. The last remnants of her troubled sleep disappeared as she followed him through the tunnel. She didn't know why the gruff wizard calmed her nerves. He didn't hug or speak to her gently. He laid no magic spell upon her. She supposed she craved company more than nourishment. That's why she had waited to eat the pheasant.

A heavy cauldron sat amidst hot red logs in the fire pit. The wizard had been expecting her. Mathair Mhór always had a fire ready along with the proper utensils needed to skin or pluck whatever prey Caer brought home.

Gallean plunged the bird into the boiling pot of water to scald the feathers, making it easier to pluck. "How did you rest last night?"

"Not well."

"And what troubles the young warrior?"

It would be easy to lie to him and not mention the truth about her past, about who was after her, but she was sure the wizard already knew.

"I was haunted by the death of my father."

He sat on a log and quickly pulled at the feathers. "You witnessed your father's death?"

Gallean's gift of sight annoyed her. Why ask questions he already knew? "You knew that, didn't you."

"I see many things," he said, spearing the pheasant with a long stick and resting it across the fire on two spikes. "But I don't see everything."

"It was a man." No, it had been too long since she even thought of him as a man. She didn't believe there was any humanity left in him, if there ever was. "He was a monster," was all she could say.

"And what did you see?"

"I saw him slice my father's throat."

"Why did you run from him?"

"I was scared. He wanted to possess me. He wanted me for his own."

"How do you know that?"

She suspected Gallean was trying to get to the root of what was troubling her, but she didn't want to go there. She couldn't. All she knew was that Balor wanted to possess her. She just knew.

Gallean adjusted the bird to roast the other side. She watched him as she thought about Balor and how she knew he wanted her.

They sat in a long silence, but it was not uncomfortable. It wasn't like the night before, when she had sat alone, longing for companionship. Finally, she spoke. "It was his eye."

"Which one?"

"The one that looked at me. I was hiding in the tunnel like a coward. Balor knew I was watching him. I wondered what was beneath the leather patch. If there was an empty eye socket or an eyeball with no pupil. Or something else. That's when he looked at me with his good eye. It was gray. Lifeless. It felt like it bored into my brain."

"And what did it see?"

"It saw a girl terrified for her father because she knew what was coming next and still hid like a coward."

Gallean poked at the hot coals to ensure a well-roasted meal. Caer thought their conversation was finished, but then in a quiet voice he said, "What did he see in you?"

Caer had already answered him. "He saw me," she said, stubbornly frustrated that he wasn't understanding what she was saying.

"But who are you?"

"I'm a girl. I am just a girl."

He turned away from the fire to face her. "Are you?"

Tears welled in her eyes. She swiped them away. "I don't know what you mean."

"I think you do," he said. His words wrapped around her and pulled her into an embrace without ever touching her. "You're tugging at those white tufts right now."

When Caer realized what she was doing, she shoved her hands beneath her legs. "What does it mean? What does it mark me as?"

Gallean's chest rose and fell. He didn't say anything for a long time, and she wondered if he would even answer her. "It marks you as different."

That she already knew. "Different in what way?"

He pursed his lips. She could tell he was deciding how much to tell her. "There is more you can do."

Her vocal cords tightened. A distant memory tried to

surface, but she forced it down. She wanted Gallean to tell her. "What else can I do?"

He tore off a leg from the bird and handed it to her. "That's not for me to reveal. It is for you discover on your own."

Her mouth watered as she studied the leg. "But what if I don't know how? What if I never know?"

He smiled at her before speaking. "You will. It was written in the stars that you will make the discovery."

Mathair Mhór used to tell her that too. After the death of her father, her life rattled with riddles.

"Your guardian said that too, didn't she?" he asked before biting into the other leg.

The mind-reading ability frustrated her, but he had confirmed what she long suspected. Neither Mathair Mhór nor Gallean knew the truth of her otherness. How was she supposed to discover it without a guide?

"In time," Gallean said, reading her thoughts again. "In time."

They spent the next several days training from morning to evening, practicing how to use the sword as an extension of the body and how to swing a blade with deadly accuracy. The dull ache of exhaustion gnawed at her muscles, but she didn't want to stop. She knew she only had until the Shadow Moon before the brother and sister arrived, and she needed to learn as much as she possibly could from Gallean. Her future was wrought with mystery. She needed to spend her present in training.

She tried not to think about what her life would be like once the brother and sister arrived. After spending almost a week with the wizard, living alone did not bring her comfort.

"Concentrate," Gallean roared. "When you don't concentrate, you put yourself at risk." He jabbed at her stomach. She parried his attack and returned her own rally of swordplay. He fell away from her as she continued to bombard him.

"Yes," he said, "that's it. Always concentrate. Do not let yourself get distracted when you are in the midst of battle."

"But—"

He came at her again, putting her on the defensive. "There are no buts. You fight to win and then you get out. Do not stay past your time. Do not underestimate their skill, and do not overestimate yours."

The sun dropped past the high wall of the keep and still they fought. Him always instructing, always attacking. Caer always coming at him with more. Her cup continued to fill, and yet, it had not run over.

She angled her sword, ready to come at him with intense concentration. She would knock the old wizard off his feet to demonstrate her mastery of the day's lesson. She rushed at his left, feinted, and went for his right. She swung at his feet, but before the blade made contact, he threw his hand at her, launching her through the air. Her body smashed against the oak tree. Her arms and legs flew backward around the tree from the impact, and the air whooshed out of her lungs. Her bottom hit the stone floor, adding further insult. When she finally caught her breath, she growled, "What the . . . ?"

He threw up his hand again. Her lips pinned together. "Somebody is here," he said in a low, deep voice that traveled through the air to her.

Fear clamped down on her chest. How could someone have passed through his three energy barriers? They kept everyone out except her.

Panic stole her regained breath. Balor. Could he have found her? She had thought his reach could not extend beyond the borders of the Land of Shadows. It had been foolish of her to suppose such. He would find her no matter how far she traveled.

"It is not your monster. You will have time to fight that one."

"Then who is it?" she hissed under her breath. He waved his hand in the air for silence. And as his faithful student, she waited for him to motion her to speak again.

He shifted his body in the direction of the main tunnel to the exterior of his keep. The very one Caer had always snuck down. The only one where entrance could be granted or denied. He tilted his head as if he could hear more clearly that way.

Caer wondered if he would shift into the bear. She had seen the bear plenty of times from a distance but had never seen the transformation from human to other.

His body stiffened. "You have to get out of here now."

Anger and sadness combined together. "Where am I to go?"

He rushed over to her. "The same place you were before. The same place that you've been hiding for many years. The very place you slept last night."

The thought of leaving him and their training was more than she was capable of. She took hold of her anger instead and prepared to wield it. "I thought you said I could stay here."

He lifted his head and inhaled. Caer did the same. "It appears that the brother and sister have arrived before they were due."

Caer's muscles tightened. Her fingers dug into the handle of the sword. Her taste of joy was ruined. The brother and sister needed to die. She firmed her grip on the handle and advanced toward the tunnel.

An invisible wall stopped her from continuing.

"You will not kill them," the wizard said in a tone that spoke of danger and violence to anyone who attempted it.

She tried to empty her head of thoughts. He must not read her intention. His mind probed hers and she struggled to push him out. Her jaw twitched with the effort.

"They will not be harmed," he murmured, almost as if he was spelling her.

She could feel when she successfully expelled him from her mind and lifted her chin in defiance, but she remained quiet, as if waiting for his instruction.

"You must not become too comfortable in your surroundings at any time," he said, his voice traveling to her. His eyes widened. The brother and sister were near. "You need to go invisible."

Rebellion bloomed within her. "I thought you said I wasn't truly invisible.

"Most people are unable to detect the difference in the energies in the air."

"Knock, knock," a male voice shouted from outside of the keep.

"Now," he growled as he approached the tunnel.

Caer pulled the energy around her and shifted into invisible. Animosity toward the brother and sister welled up inside her. They had arrived ahead of schedule, ruining her training and destroying her one chance at learning how to protect herself from the monster who hunted her. She wanted to kill them. It mattered not that Gallean had said they were the only ones that could help her. They needed to be destroyed. She'd risk Gallean's punishment. It would pale in comparison with what Balor had planned for her.

The years between her father's death and now had been long. Not a moment could be wasted. The brother and sister must be eliminated.

11

DID YOU SEE THAT?

J'm completely expecting to see Madigan standing before us with his hands shoved in his pockets and his proverbial tail shoved between his legs, but I don't see him. Not one freaking part of him.

"Are you still here?" Scott shouts, thinking that maybe Madigan hid behind a tree or crawled under a rock or something.

Just when a reincarnated goddess thinks it's safe to go outside, some new mystical being or magical ability reveals itself. Er, in this case, doesn't reveal himself.

"I'm here," he says. We both jump because he sounds like he's literally right next to us.

Scott was one of those kids who wanted to touch everything when Uncle Mark, now known as "Dad," took us shopping. I did too, but while Scott was the kid everyone smiled at and gave a lollipop to because he was just so darn cute and would only "look with his eyes," I was the reason there were signs posted that said, "Keep an eye on your children" and "If you break it, you bought it." But Scott's the one dying to get his hands on Madigan. Who gets the lollipop now?

"Can I, um . . . do you mind if I reach out and try to touch you?" Scott says to the empty space in front of us. It would be a creepy request if it wasn't Scott asking with wide-eyed, childlike amazement.

"Sure. I've never had anybody ask me that before. Truth is, I've never told anybody I could do this before."

His confession makes me realize just how much trust and faith he's placed in us as well.

Scott slowly reaches his hands out. You know when you wake up at night and have to go to the bathroom, but you don't want to turn on the light and blind yourself, so you sorta zombie-walk and wind up smashing your toe? He looks just like that. One by one he extends his fingers. Then he extends his arms, but not fully, because he winds up finding Madigan. "Oh my gods," he says under his breath. "Wow."

The wonder in his voice makes me want to reach out and touch Madigan too. Especially since the space in front of me doesn't look like a single person is there. It's just nothing-ness. And Madigan is definitely not breakable.

"Can I touch?"

"Yeah, sure," Madigan says, sounding much braver than he does when he's visible. I guess if I could become invisible, I might be braver too. I reach out both hands, and since my arms are shorter than Scott's, I wind up going full Franken-stein's monster and shuffle forward before smacking right into him.

He yelps in surprise as I fall backward, landing on my ass.

"Are you okay?" Two giant hands wrap around my twiggy arms, and it's my turn to yelp because there's no body—or face or hands for that matter—because he is fecking invisible.

I let Madigan help me up since I'm kinda in shock. Not regular Madigan, but invisible Madigan, which makes it even cooler. "Holy shit! That's awesome. How do you do that?"

I stare at the space where Madigan would be standing.

Patterns of energy, albeit invisible energy, swirl around where his body is supposed to be. I reach out and touch the energy field, forgetting that there's a real person standing there and not a magical anomaly.

He laughs. "Hey, that's my stomach."

I snap my hand back. "Oops, sorry."

"That was rude," Scott says indignantly.

Surprise, surprise. Now that Madigan possesses a super-hero ability, Scott trusts him completely. Or at least thinks Madigan's worth more effort. Frankly, the only way Madigan could be any cooler in Scott's eyes now would be if he turned green. Scott also harbors a Hulk crush.

"Like you didn't do it too. Madigan, can you reappear just as easily?"

As soon as I finish my question, he appears in front of us.

"Wow," Scott says again. He's a man of limited vocabulary this afternoon. Lucky for all of us, I've got my wits about me.

"How do you disappear?"

Madigan purses his lips. I try to get a read on him. I know it's wrong, but hey, if you had mind-reading abilities, wouldn't you use them too?

Eventually, after trying to put an explanation into words, he lifts his shoulders. "I dunno."

Scott's still tongue-tied, so I continue peppering him with questions. "How did you discover you could do it? How old were you?"

His face darkens. The cheerful guy disappears, replaced by a sad one.

"Apologies for Gigi. She asks wildly inappropriate and often too personal questions. You don't have to tell us if you're not comfortable with it."

He shoves his hands in his pockets. "It's okay. I trust you. It's just that it trudges up my past, and I haven't thought about my old family for a long time."

So many questions, but before I can ask another one, Scott pipes back in. "Not to be a jerk or anything, but why didn't you tell us about the skill from the very beginning? All those times you went to their house to fetch clothing—you were always invisible, weren't you."

Again Madigan looks sheepish. "You knew I was a werewolf, and we didn't talk about that."

"Yeah, but why didn't you say something before?"

Madigan reaches down and picks up a rock. He lobs it back and forth between his hands. "It's just that . . . my parents didn't approve. They thought I was a changeling swapped out for their baby because one time when my ma was changing my diaper, I disappeared. They thought I was a fairy baby, and that fairies stole their real baby to be their servant. They blamed me any time anything went missing. One day, I was but five or six, my da tried to punish me for stealing some bread. I disappeared before he could lay a hand on me and left."

Scott and I both reach out our hands for him and send him soothing thoughts. I think of the time we both touched Ryan when he was in the hospital. We didn't realize it then, but I think we pushed calmness into him too.

"Were you born a werewolf?"

Gi, do you think it's really the best time to ask?

Yes, I do.

"Carman found me wandering the countryside. She made me believe that . . ." he hesitates.

Sure, I'd spent some time with Carman, and of course she'd helped raise Alaric, but that was the extent of my knowledge. Anything we could learn about her could help us figure out what to do with Maria. "What, Madigan?"

"That I could become part of their family since my own abandoned me. All I had to do was . . ."

Scott and I lean forward. I know Alaric's werewolf origin

story—his mother was impregnated by Clayone. But I don't know anyone else's. Carman's manual provided details of the different ways to make a werewolf, but after seeing the dungeons and the claw marks in the cells, and with the stench of death hanging heavy, I'd guess there were far more failures than successes.

One of her successes was standing in front of us.

Scott rubs his hands together in an effort to change the subject. As much as he wants to know Madigan's creation story, he thinks it might be too soon. Madigan revealing his invisibility was enough. "How about we grab a bite to eat and unload for a while."

Madigan smiles. "I appreciate you trying to distract me, but let's try to find Alaric first. He's my alpha. I need him."

"He's your best friend too, isn't he."

"'Tis true." A lone tear trails down his massive cheek. "Let's get on with it then," he says cheerfully, as if his disappearing act revelation had no impact on Scott and me whatsoever. I guess he's right too. Now that he's out of the invisibility closet, there's nothing left to do but find Alaric.

I poke the fire to get it going. Once it's flaming to my satisfaction, I spread the map and Alaric's shirt out on the ground, then begin chanting the tracking spell. I've done it so many times now that I know it by memory, but this time, I add my own words into it. They sort of slip from my brain and out of my mouth before I can regret messing up the spell. Out of the mist of my mind appear the dungeons next to Saint Brigit's Cathedral I glance at the map to verify that Alaric is indeed trapped in the dungeons.

"But I didn't see him," I whisper aloud. "I didn't feel him."

Scott places his hand on my shoulder and shoots a burst of truthful energy into me. "If you think about it, it makes sense. You cloaked Breas. Maybe they clocked Alaric so that not even Clarissa could find him. I mean, Breas is a god and all. He's got to be far more powerful than we are, though I hate admitting that. Maybe you and I don't know enough magic to override really powerful magic."

"Do you think Maria is powerful enough to cast such a spell?" Madigan says.

Scott shrugs. "She could be if she was trained by Carman, but she's still really young. I don't know a lot about magical training, but it seems that magic grows with time. Gigi and I haven't spent enough time learning it. Not yet at least."

Hopeful optimism fills the air around us. It's the first time Scott solidly believes we'll get control of our magic. That we can use it for good and not deep-sea diving with tourists.

Madigan kicks dirt into the fire. He's a man of action. He tires of our long-winded conversations. "Well let's stop yammering and go get Alaric."

I like his style. "He's got a point there. Do we need anything? Axes, pitchforks, that sort of thing?"

"What you need," Granda says, appearing before us, "is a powerful wizard."

"And an ancient witch," Clarissa adds.

I fold back up the map and hand it to Scott. "Surprise, surprise. You've known what we were up to all along, haven't you."

"Of course," they say together without a hint of remorse or embarrassment about watching over us.

"We knew you'd find Alaric eventually," Granda says.

"So, let's have a go," Madigan says.

We take the entrance to the dungeons Clarissa found the night that Alaric went missing. The one far away from Saint Brigit's Cathedral. The one, come to think of it, much closer to Carman's cottage than to Granda's. Even with her gone, she's still impacting our lives.

As we approach the entrance, Clarissa puts her hands out to stop us. "Wait," she says, then murmurs something. A small light appears in front of her and shoots into the entrance.

"What's that for?" Scott whispers.

"That's to check for any traps that may be waiting for us," she says.

"Well, are there?" he replies.

The light flies back at us and disappears into Clarissa's hand. "There do not appear to be. But be cautious. Carman is extremely powerful."

"Carman is dead," I say, but as soon as the words leave my mouth, I don't believe it.

"She's alive and well," Granda says.

"She's Maria, isn't she." Scott says. "Gigi's the one who normally makes bad hookup choices. Is it disgusting that I tried to get a piece of Maria?"

Granda pats his shoulder. "If it's any consolation, the mind is under Carman's control. The body very much belongs to the poor girl she possessed."

Scott shakes his head. "I don't think that makes me feel better."

That's why I sensed conflict in Maria when we met at Hell's Gate. The real Maria's voice kept trying to be heard. She wanted to get out. "Can we expel Carman from her?"

Clarissa takes my hand. "Do not worry about the girl's spirit. It will only distract you. Amorin and I will attend to that complication."

"It sounds like more than a complication."

When Lizzie bought the eyeball necklace from that scary dude at the flea market, her behavior changed, and the stupid eyeball necklace was the cause of it. The spell book definitely didn't help, but it was the necklace that changed her. Was that Carman's all-seeing eyeball? That would explain why I wanted nothing to do with it. It would also explain the whole freaky-exorcism-pagan-ritual in the school's attic that included Kensey getting tortured. When the candles went out, I had swiped the necklace from Lizzie. I broke the connection without even knowing it. And without the spell book, Carman lost all contact with her. I buried that cursed piece of jewelry deep in the woods behind Gram's house. If I ever return to Vernal Falls, I'll bind the ground so the freaky eyeball can never be used again.

"If it's any consolation, the girl allowed Carman entrance. Permission is usually needed for the possession to work," Clarissa says.

But it's no consolation at all, because that would mean Lizzie, my dear sweet Lizzie, had allowed Carman to enter her too.

Scott and I walk into the tunnel in front of the others. The idea of someone granting permission for an evil spirit to possess them weighs heavily on both of us. Scott doesn't know about the Lizzie-Carman possession situation. He's concerned for the real Maria and wondering what he can do to help her. All amorous feelings about her are gone—he worries for the girl's soul.

Then I realize why Maria was so familiar to me. She was the girl at Carman's bonfire. The one who wanted the boy to fall in love with her—the boy who'd tried to fight Scott that night at Hell's Gate. How could I have been so stupid? I should have sensed something was up. *Someone* should have told me.

Way to beat around the bush. It wasn't my place to.

It's never your place.

A discussion for another time.

Always another time.

Alaric . . .

Fine.

Just so I feel like I'm doing something and to distract

myself, I send out feelers of my own to see if there are any remaining remnants of magic in the tunnel. Thankfully, there don't appear to be. We wander down to the main cavern area together.

Madigan inhales deeply. "There have been new were-wolves in here recently. Strange smells that I can't place."

I look over at the wall mural of Alaric with Clayone watching over him along with the rest of Clayone's pack. "Are there any you do recognize?"

He inhales again. "Declan, for sure. Maria, definitely. And some of my other mates, but there are a whole bunch of others I don't know at all."

He sounds scared.

I rest my hand on his arm to calm him. "You can go invisible if you want."

Granda and Clarissa gasp. "He can go invisible?"

Their surprise worries me. They've been around a long time. They've experienced loads of magic. Especially Clarissa —aka the nineteenth nun of the Druid Sisters of the Gallicenial, aka the Flame Keeper. The reason for their surprise could be as simple as finding a person gifted with invisibility or—and believe me, I hate even going there—there's another part of a prophecy or a new prophecy that affects us all.

"Do I even want to know?"

"It's not important now," Granda says as if reassuring himself as well as us. "But if you must, go invisible."

With Granda's permission, Madigan pulls the space around him and disappears. While Clarissa and Granda gawk over his ability, I wander over to Alaric's image.

"Scott? Can you come here for second?"

Scott stands beside me. "What's up?"

"Can you lift me up on your shoulders?"

He bends down and I climb onto his back. "Somebody

you wanna play chicken with? I can't say it's the appropriate time or place."

I tap the top of his head as he stands up. "No, I just want to look up close. I don't even have a picture of him."

The wall shimmers in front of me, but that may be the tears blurring my vision at the sight of Alaric. I reach to press my hand against the wall.

"Gigi, don't!" Granda and Clarissa shout together, but it's too late. My hand firmly covers Alaric one second and then disappears along with the rest of me the next.

AND DOWN THEY GO

Scott stands up, brushing leaves and other debris off his pants. "What the hell just happened? Where are we?"

I push myself off the ground. "I don't know."

Nervous energy swirls around him. I step away because if he falls into one of his magical episodes, I could be in trouble.

"You're the one who touched the mural. You're the one who dropped us into . . ." he looks around, trying to figure out where we are, but the trees, the grass, and the rocks don't exactly nail down a specific location, except that it's not in the large cavern with Clarissa, Granda, and Madigan. "What is this? A portal? Did we fall into a portal?"

Before I can answer, before I can even breathe, he launches into a tirade.

"That's exactly what happened. We fell into a portal. But where? How? I'm sure you were doing your magic thing when you were staring up at Alaric's image. You probably didn't even know what you were doing when you did it. I let you climb up on my shoulders to get a better view, and when you touched the picture—because you just had to touch it, because that's who you are—we fell through a portal."

The air above him begins to circle around. It's been a while since he created his own personal tornado, but that's exactly what he's doing. And since I have no idea where we are or what type of danger we're in, he needs to get his shit together.

"Scott, calm down. It's not my fault."

He looks at me with that skepticism that suggests it is one hundred percent my fault.

"Okay, so maybe it is. Let me just take a second to figure out where we are."

"Where we are is screwed," Scott says.

"Not helpful." I glare at him one more time for good measure before skimming the horizon for clues.

"True. Okay, let me just . . ." he says. I squint my eyes at him, hoping that maybe this time red laser beams shoot out of them. He bats the imaginary lasers away. "All right, I'll try to calm down. It's just—you know I'm not really good in situations I don't have any control over."

"One would think you'd be used to it by now. You've been hanging out with me since birth. I've been putting you in situations that are out of your comfort zone for our entire life."

He nods along with me. "True. That is definitely true. This last month has been especially bizarre. And now this?" The tornado starts to pick up again.

"Still not helpful."

"Okay, you're right." He starts walking around, as if that will help him figure out where we are, but it annoys the crap out of me. Especially when I'm trying to concentrate. He keeps talking anyway, because that is who he is—he can't help blabbing. "So we're thinking we fell through a portal. Maybe it's like the Harry Potter kind of thing. We grab a boot, or in this case Alaric's ass—don't think I wasn't watching—then we get zapped to another place. The question is, where?"

"Thank you, Scott, for stating the obvious. That's exactly what *I'm* trying to figure out, but it's impossible with your nonstop yapping."

He keeps walking like he doesn't even hear me. He's deep in thought about how we got here. "Or," he says, "remember when Mrs. Weasley throws Floo powder on Harry before he enters the fireplace, and he needs to fully think about where he's going or he'll wind up Splinched?"

I throw my hands up in the air. I mean, really, what else am I supposed to do? "Again with the Harry Potter references. Is it really necessary? I'm not Splinched. And you, unfortunately, always look like that. Splinching might have been an improvement. And for your information, Splinching only happens when a person doesn't Apparate correctly. And Floo powder gets thrown into the fireplace, not on Harry. If you're going to rely on fictionalized magical encounters, at least get them right."

He nods as he paces around, lost in thought. My jab flies right over his head. He actually reminds me of Newt Scamander in *Fantastic Beasts*, but no way am I telling him that. It'll only encourage him more. "Yes, yes, that's what happened," he says to himself as he scratches his head. "Yes, exactly." He blinks and returns to this world—wherever that may be. "Okay, since Voldemort, or in this case Carman, hasn't revealed I to us yet, let's assume we fell through a portal. What were you thinking about when you touched Alaric's ass?"

The ground suddenly becomes fascinating to me. I don't want to tell him. I really don't.

"Gigi, whatever you were thinking about could be the key

to explaining where we are. Maybe even what dimension we're in."

He's right, but I hate admitting the truth to him because it makes me seem like a horrible, self-absorbed person—even more so than what he probably already thinks I am.

Deep breaths, Gigi. Deep breaths.

"I was thinking about Alaric. About how much I wanted to find him. Then I felt guilty that I didn't want to find Lizzie with the same intensity. When I touched his image, I was thinking about him again. And then, all of a sudden, I was thinking about how to find him. And then we fell through the portal."

Scott glances around. The sun's making its way to the horizon. We're on a small hill in an open meadow with trees and rocks in the distance. His tornado's pretty much completely gone, thank the gods.

"Well, we are definitely on another fairy mound. So that portal . . . whoever left it there wanted us to land here, but I don't think we're in Newgrange or Kildare. It still seems like Ireland though, but what Ireland? Or where in Ireland?"

"Kildare and Newgrange are not the only places that have fairy mounds, brainiac." Arguing with him makes me feel more comfortable with my surroundings.

"Who's not being helpful now?"

"You've got a point, but where do you think we are?"

He looks out across the horizon. "If I had to guess. We're either in a very large seomra de rúin or we're actually at Gallean's."

I follow his gaze. In the distance I can see smoke spiraling out of the chimney of what appears to be a small stone keep. "How can that be? The Shadow Moon isn't for three days."

Scott turns to me. "Gigi, we're reincarnated gods. Nobody actually knows what we're capable of. The rules that Clarissa, Granda, and even Gallean follow apply to mortals and magical beings. But honestly, we are so much more than that. Clarissa and Granda thought we had to wait until the Shadow Moon, but I think godly powers trump astrology. Or in this case, your godly powers."

I'm not willing to admit that I messed things up for us again, so I settle on distraction. "What about Madigan? We were just making progress with him. What's going to happen to him now that we're here? What about Granda and Clarissa? And my tracking spell for Alaric actually worked. What about finding him?"

Scott climbs down the fairy mound toward Gallean's keep. "They'll work it out. Maybe Madigan will stay invisible the entire time we're gone. Or maybe he'll go live with Granda for a while and keep him company. As for your tracking spell to find Alaric . . ." he glances over my shoulder to make sure I'm coming, "that's probably what got us here."

I'm amazed that he's so relaxed about the entire situation now that he has calmed down and is thinking rationally. I wish some of it would rub off on me. Instead, fear spawns in my gut. I sprint to catch up to him. "The tracking spell led us to the dungeons. Do you think we were cursed? Do you think Carman laid a magical trap for us?"

He elbows me. "Sorta like the trophy in *The Goblet of Fire*."

I elbow him back in a not-so-polite response.

"The truth is, Gi, we're not going to know. But, I don't think a witch, no matter how powerful or how evil, can create a portal into another dimension. I think you did that. I think you did it because you were thinking about finding Alaric, and I think that you sent us here."

"But Alaric isn't in the Shadow Realm. He's in the Earthly Realm—er, is that what we should call it?"

Scott doesn't seem to think that this is all that out of the ordinary. "Sure. And maybe he isn't here, but maybe it's the only way to find him."

I elbow him again. He winces, rubbing his side. Pointy elbows have their advantages. "Oh my gods, Scott. Are you going all-knowing-godlike on me? Because if you are, I am going to kick your ass."

"No, I'm just being practical about it. You know magic. I know magic. But we barely have control over our powers. Maybe you need to learn some special skills in order to find Alaric. Or maybe you'll discover a special spell in the Shadow Realm that allows you to harness the power to find him."

"Or protect myself from a pack of angry werewolves at the next full moon because they all think I killed Alaric."

He waves his hand in the air, dismissing the notion that I could possibly be in any danger. "I wouldn't worry about the pack if I were you. That Maria, even if she is Carman, can be dealt with. She doesn't scare me whatsoever."

"Easy for you to say. She hasn't had a vendetta against you for fifteen hundred years."

"You've got a point there. But still, not scary. I'm mean, she did fall for my charms for at least a little while when we were dancing at Hell's Gate."

I roll my eyes. "She was acting."

He pats the top of my head. "No one can act *that* well. Trust me."

We pass through a protective wall of energy. Our bodies tingle, but it doesn't knock us on our asses like the one at Newgrange.

"Gallean must use these to keep out intruders."

He pokes through the wall we just passed with his finger. "Doesn't appear to keep out welcomed guests or imprison them either."

"I'm not sure if we're welcome." I'm definitely not feeling the Gallean love, that's for sure.

"Oh, don't be a poor sport again just because I found my key much faster than you."

"It took me hours to find it."

"Whatever. You survived. Think of it as character building."

"Speaking of character building, now that you know Maria isn't some teenage girl you were looking to get a piece of . . ."

He throws up his hands. "Hold up, I wasn't trying to get into her pants. She was trying to get into mine."

"You totally were."

"Well, maybe."

"I thought you were saving yourself for your swan."

"From what everybody tells me, I won't find her until I shed my mortality and return to the Otherworld. I don't know about you, but I'm not planning to pick up a full-time residency in the Otherworld anytime soon."

"No, definitely not."

"Exactly. I've got years—maybe decades—before I rejoin my true love. Am I supposed to wait around for her, or am I allowed to have some fun? Being the God of Love, I feel it's my obligation to have some fun."

"Looking for any excuse to get some action."

"Maybe."

"Following the stereotype that gods are sex-crazed lunatics?"

"Takes one to know one."

I shove him through another energy field. "I was referring to Breas."

He pulls me through. "Right, Breas."

We pass through one more energy field on our way to Gallean's keep. In the seomra de rúin we only saw the keep from the inside. But somehow, when Scott saw the outside of it today, he just knew what it was.

The high stone walls keep out as many uninvited guests as I suspect they keep in. That's if Gallean's bear persona doesn't scare the holy crud out of anyone who attempts to approach the keep. I'm not looking forward to meeting the bear again, but then again, I always get along better with animals than people, so who knows? Maybe this will be a "Come to Gigi" moment for us both.

"Do you hear that?" Scott says in a low voice. "It sounds like he's talking to somebody."

The quiet muttering fills the empty spaces left in the silence of the early evening. "Maybe he's talking to himself like you do. Don't think I haven't noticed."

He stops and listens. "No, no! He's definitely talking to someone."

I peek down the long tunnel to the courtyard of the keep, but before I can get a good look, Scott pulls me back against the wall.

"That's rude."

"Says the eavesdropper. Listen, if he doesn't want to be observed, then he ought to shut the doors." I point at the hulking wooden doors standing open on either side of the tunnel.

"I'm not really sure what the protocol is when you enter an all-powerful sorcerer's lair."

"I'm pretty sure he's a wizard. Sorcerer sounds too Disney. Just knock."

"Knock, knock," he shouts.

Gallean, in wizard form, appears in the opening at the end of the tunnel. He looks at us for a long time. So long, in fact, that I kinda wish the bear had shown up. Finally he says, "The Shadow Moon is not for another three days. How is it you've arrived?"

"We've been asking ourselves that same question for the past half hour," Scott says. "I blame Gigi. She always finds the loophole to most situations. But such as it is, we're here now."

I watch the wizard closely. He's not shifting into a bear, but he's not pleased with our presence. I don't mean to be cocky, but we are reincarnated gods, and that doesn't happen very often, so I don't know why he would be hesitant about letting us into his keep. He should be welcoming us with open arms. Maybe even throwing a party. Or at least tossing a handful of confetti.

Scott picks up on Gallean's hesitation too. "Is it bad timing? Are you otherwise engaged?"

Gallean puts his back to us, which is pretty rude, especially since he keeps talking. "It's fine. Clarissa and Amorin did not inform me of your early arrival."

I keep my mouth shut. It's probably best to let Scott do all the talking. He likes to do that anyway.

"We left rather unexpectedly."

"Will the story be long?" Gallean asks, sounding bored. I get that we're early, but geez, isn't he the least bit curious about how we got here? He keeps glancing around the keep as if he's looking for someone or something to save him from a long, drawn-out tale. I'm guessing either Granda gave him a heads up on our banter or he's lived by himself for so long that he has no patience for conversation of any kind. Scott and I will be a challenge in many different respects to him.

"Gigi was thinking about her missing boyfriend. She touched a painting of him, and we disappeared and wound up here."

"Remarkable," Gallean says to himself. "Quite remarkable."

My stomach growls, reminding me that we haven't eaten since breakfast. "Not to be rude, but we conducted a tracking spell, which led us on a search for the missing boyfriend and inadvertently traveled through a portal to wind up here, and we haven't eaten all day. We're starving."

Gallean strolls over to his fire pit. The picked-over

remains of what appears to be some kind of bird cling to a roasting stick. "Of course," he says, sliding the bones into the fire.

I watch the flames consume the rather large carcass. He is a sizable man, but that's a lot of meat for one person even if he is a bear.

"Are you sure we aren't interrupting anything?"

A sheen of sweat drips from his brow, but it's not from the heat of the fire. What was he doing before we got there?

He pokes the coals with a long, rather intimidating iron poker. "No, definitely not. Let me get you something." He disappears inside his keep.

Meanwhile, Scott makes himself comfortable on the same bench he sat at in the seomra de rúin when I was too busy finding a key to sit. I have the strangest feeling that somebody else is standing in the courtyard with us. I keep looking around, but I don't see anyone.

Gallean returns with dried strips of meat, cheese, and bread. I'm guessing there aren't many vegetarians in the Shadow Realm.

"Are you sure we aren't interrupting? I feel like someone else is here."

In the far corner of the keep, next to the tunnel where Gallean appeared after he shifted into a man from a bear, I swear I see an energy field similar to Madigan's.

Gallean steps in front of me, effectively blocking my view before glancing over both of his shoulders in an exaggerated, almost comical motion. "Nobody but me."

His reaction and his entire body language are out of character. Not that we became best friends during our first visit, but he definitely seemed more serious then.

"Whatever you say," I mumble under my breath and tear off a piece of bread with my fingers.

As Scott engages him in conversation, I worry about our

early arrival. I don't know how long we'll be in the Shadow Realm, or what we'll learn, or even how we'll even get back to the Earthly Realm. I hope that the time away from our search for Alaric and Lizzie doesn't mean the end of their lives. I don't want to continue finding and losing Alaric again and again in each of my reincarnations. I want to be able to be with him in this one.

You will, Gigi. You will.

13

NINE OF WANDS

*A*nger boiled in Caer's veins, promising to erupt at the slightest provocation, for she desired revenge above all else. With the brother and sister's early arrival, her training had abruptly ended. She did not dispute that the skills she'd learned over the past few days would assist her when she went up against Balor, but she needed more. Going against the enemy ill-equipped would lead to an early death, and though she wasn't afraid of dying, she didn't want to.

Gallean had insisted that she stand in the far corner. Initially it rankled her to be forced into hiding, but it would prove an effective vantage point to determine which one to dispatch first. Regardless of the wizard's warning about not killing them, she'd end them both.

He led the pair into the keep, much the same as he had done for her after he'd made himself known to her. She was surprised at the size of the sister. She was much smaller than Caer remembered. Her behavior in the battle with the bear and her indignant search for the key had made her seem much larger, more of a comparable opponent. But now, watching her enter the keep, Caer wasn't sure how she had even gotten to the Land of Shadows, let alone why Gallean had agreed to train her. She was unimpressive in every way. She didn't even carry a sword, bow, or weapons belt. She'd prove an easy target.

The brother continued to apologize to Gallean for their early arrival. He didn't know how they had arrived before the Shadow Moon, but the prospect of training with the wizard brought light to his persona. His eyes sparkled with excitement, even with his apologies. She'd forgotten the way the brother's appearance made parts of her body tingle. She supposed, had she not wanted to kill him, she would have considered him handsome. Now he just stood in the way of her survival.

He constantly adjusted his body to ensure he could protect his sister if Gallean were to attack. His strong build and quick feet demonstrated a high level of physical prowess. He would not be easy to kill even if he was untrained.

Auras shimmered around each of them, hinting that they were more than they appeared to be. Her initial assessment of the sister had been false. She was powerful even without weapons. The sister may not be able to conduct magic in the Land of Shadows, but her skills would develop and surpass the brother's with very little training.

Gallean led them over to the fire. The sister took Caer's seat from earlier and the brother sat nearby. Gallean had told her that they were the only two who could help her. Caer would not take that chance. She couldn't risk them gaining power as a result of Gallean's training when he ought to be training her. She'd kill the sister first, then worry about the brother.

She gripped the handle of her sword. It would serve her well. Once the brother and sister were gone, Gallean would thank her, and then they could proceed with her studies. With the wizard's back to her, she took a step toward them. The sister glanced in her direction. She couldn't have heard Caer move—Caer prided herself on her stealth—but she squinted her eyes all the same and studied the space. If she had gained mastery of some of her abilities, she might be able to see Caer as Gallean had.

Caer thought about slicing the sister's throat just as Balor had done to her father. But if the sister jerked at all, or if the brother intervened, there was a possibility that the sister could remain alive. So the head then.

With a dull blade, one needed exact precision and tremendous effort to ensure success. Caer sharpened her blades every day. If the motion was swift and true, the head would cut clear off. With the element of surprise on her side and the wizard occupied in conversation, she raised her arms above her head, sword at the ready, and stalked toward the sister.

Without even looking in Caer's direction, Gallean placed himself in front of the sister, blocking her line of attack. Caer adjusted her position and leapt at her.

The wizard shifted around to face her. Without him muttering a word or making any marked movement, an invisible prison locked around her, effectively immobilizing her in attack position, arms raised over her head, legs outstretched in a long stride.

Neither the brother nor the sister were phased by Gallean turning his back on them, nor did they sense that their lives had been threatened. Even the sister ceased looking in Caer's direction. She guessed the wizard had laid an additional protection of invisibility on her. He didn't want the brother or the sister to discover his other student's presence any more than Caer wanted them in the Land of Shadows.

Her joints ached as she stood frozen, forced to watch the brother and sister plead for nourishment after she had provided a plump pheasant each morning since her training began. They were worse than the beggars she came across in the village.

The wizard cast a glance in her direction on his way into the kitchen. His eyes promised punishment at the next available opportunity, and though she didn't like being unable to move, she knew it was better than whatever retribution the wizard would take.

He soon returned with a heaping plate of meats, bread, and cheese for his new guests. She watched with disgust as the sister tore bread apart with her fingers before eating it, as if it was too much effort to rip it off with her teeth. To Caer, it was a sign of weakness and inhospitality. The wizard didn't seem to agree. The manner in which he studied the brother and sister's every action and reaction suggested he was preparing to be their teacher.

He called them by their forenames, Scott and Gigi. Neither name hinted at legendary power. Not like Cu Chulainn, the great warrior Mathair Mhór had raised long before Caer came to live with her. He was a man worthy of the bards' affections. Perhaps someday she would be too, but it wasn't the promise of legends and myth that drove her.

Soon after the meal, the brother and sister hinted at their exhaustion and need for rest. Gallean cast a shrewd glance at Caer before leading them to the opposite end of the keep, most likely to one of the rooms he had offered her only days before. She had chosen not to stay because of her need for solitude in order to reflect on what the wizard had shared with her. Now, she regretted her decision. Either the brother or the sister would be sleeping in the very bed she had planned to stay in tonight if the wizard had offered again.

The loss of a night's sleep in a bed added another blow to

her already bruised ego. It had been years since she'd slept in one. The nest of pine boughs, branches, and leaves she had created in the cave provided an adequate night's sleep, but it was nothing like the warmth and the comfort she had experienced in her own bed at Mathair Mhór's cottage.

She keenly felt the many losses of her life at that moment. The wizard casting her away when something shiny and new appeared was the crushing blow. Tears streamed down her face. The most awful part of the immobilization was that she couldn't swipe them off. They etched streaks across her cheeks as they trailed down her lips and into her throat.

Soon Gallean returned. He didn't shift into the bear, although he was more terrifying now than the shocking beast had ever been.

"You almost killed the only two who can help you," he growled.

More tears fell down her face. This time for the disappointment reflected in the wizard's eyes. Being frozen, she didn't think she could speak, but she had to try. He had to understand.

As if reading her thoughts, he waved his hand, freeing her lips.

"I need you to train me, but with them here, my training is finished," she burst out.

"You will watch just as you have for many years."

It was a cruel reminder that he had known of her presence from the very beginning. All those nights when she'd cried herself to sleep . . . and other nights, when she couldn't sleep because of monsters in the dark—both real and imagined. She would have savored every moment with the wizard had he taken her in instead of the brother and sister. The training she would have received by his side would have prepared her for every foe she'd ever encounter, but her fate had changed.

"After their arrival in the seomra de rúin, you shifted from warrior training to that bizarre energy dance. A dance will not save me. I do not possess magic. I do not have the skills that you do. I do not have the ability to manipulate energy and use it to my advantage."

His eyes skewered her where she stood. "You possess your own forms of power. Just as powerful. Just as dangerous."

She wished she could move. The emotion filling her throat almost choked her. "Then train me!"

"It is my duty to teach them. I've agreed to it, and I do not go back on my word."

Caer read between the lines. Understanding dawned on her. "And there's no duty to teach me. I get it. I'm disposable. Toss me out as you did the carcass of the pheasant I brought you this morning. What did they bring you? They will only take. They do not know how to give."

He crossed his arms, resembling the warrior she believed him to be. "And what is it that you know of them?"

"I know that my training has ended before it even began, and that is enough."

The wizard stood for a long time. She could tell he wrestled with what he should share with her and what he should keep locked away. She wished he would get on with it already. The ache in every one of her frozen muscles would break her before whatever it was he had to say did.

"The three of you possess your own forms of power. To unite the *trí cumhacht*, the three powers, is to put the circle at risk."

To suggest that the three of them were connected and bound together in some way went beyond her comprehension.

"You mustn't try to kill the sister or the brother again. If your attempt at harm had succeeded, it would have brought disgrace upon me."

The venom in his voice slithered over her. Her face grew hot with the shame of it, but like the petulant child, she couldn't let him see her embarrassment. "I didn't succeed, though, did I?"

"No, and you won't have the opportunity to do it again. You must rid yourself of this place before the brother and sister discover you."

"I thought you said I could observe you training them."

"The sister has detected your energy. I was able to add another layer, but I will be unable to if I'm distracted with their training. You will watch from outside the keep, just as before."

"Dismissed to hide in the shadows," she said. Now that she had been brought into the light, the thought of returning to the darkness filled her with bitterness. "I'd rather perish on my own than be forced to hide again."

At this point Caer would've stomped off, but she was still immobilized by Gallean. Frustration at not being able to escape roared through her. "Unleash me," she growled.

The wizard's eyes softened as he waved his hand. "I wish I'd had more time to train you before they arrived."

She dropped her arms and shook out her stiff legs. "Why do I need to be separated from them?"

"It's not so much that I'm trying to keep them away from you. I'm trying to keep you away from them. Your futures are aligned, but the universe has not blessed it yet."

The wizard frustrated her. How could he not see the truth of it? "I disagree. The universe wants us together. That's why they showed up just when my training had begun."

"True. Then perhaps it is I who is not ready for the three

of you to be joined together. I do not know if I can tame the potential power of the trí cumhacht."

"Then I'll rid myself of you and them," she said, disappearing into the night. She would not hide in the shadows any longer. She would present herself to the brother and sister. The wizard would have no choice but to train them together.

14

COOL CASE OF BS

*T*he old wizard was acting strange, constantly pacing, flinging his hands in the air for no apparent reason, behaving like we took him away from something and he was anxious to get back to it. It started last night as Scott and I gnawed on the dried beef and stale bread he gave us as our dinner—and I use that term lightly. And now, with the same rustic food for breakfast (oh joy) he'll wear a circle into the stone by the time we're done eating. I'm not one to judge someone for acting outside the definition of "normal." It's one of my life's missions to be different from everybody else, either on purpose or by accident, but he just might be something else entirely.

I pop another grape into my mouth, opting to skip the desiccated mystery meat, and trying not to long for the scones that Alaric gave me on our first morning together—when everything between us was new and wonderful, and we were just a boy and a girl falling for each other without the knowledge that one of us was a reincarnated goddess and the other was a werewolf, and—holy feck! Carman made the scones. I never thought about that before, but she must have.

Is it possible she bewitched me like Breas did with the biscuits? Were my feelings for Alaric even real, or did she spell me into caring about him and then it just felt so natural I continued?

No. NO. I'm not going to start doubting our feelings for each other. His love for me and my love for him are real. Those memories of prior lives together are real, and I will not question them. I will not corrupt them the way Carman corrupted everything else. My nails dig into my palms as I think about all the things I wish I could do to that witch if only my goddess side would allow it.

I stare off at the far corner of the keep. Last night I swear I saw someone standing there, albeit invisible. Initially I thought it was Madigan, and that somehow he came through the portal with us. But Gallean's energy barriers would have kept him out—unless the ability to become invisible makes someone immune to magic . . .

But Madigan would have eventually revealed himself to at least one of us after Gallean showed us to our rooms. And I could have sworn I heard Gallean talking to someone in the courtyard before I fell asleep. Maybe it was the girl I sensed in the seomra de rúin.

Or I'm going insane and sitting here is only making it worse. I shove the plate away from me.

"Let's get on with the training, shall we?"

Gallean stops in front of me. "You must bolster your energy with fuel before you begin. I'll not have you wallowing during a session. You can watch us while you finish eating."

I reach for a block of cheese and gnaw on it while Scott and Gallean begin a complicated dance of lifting and pushing away a ball of energy. They rise and fall in rhythm with each other. So much for actually learning anything important.

"Dance moves for the next *America's Got Talent* aren't

going to protect anyone from werewolves, rogue gods, or evil Fomorians."

Scott stops, ready to defend Gallean and his dancing feet. Gallean gestures for Scott to continue before responding to me. "I am not sure what *America's Got Talent* is, but I assure you that while you lounge around eating your breakfast, Scott and I are in every sense preparing for battle."

I snort. I had no idea wizards could be so wildly entertaining. "And just how are these moves able to combat mortal enemies?"

Gallean stiffens.

I might have gone too far, but what can I say? The wizard brings out the bitchiness in me. I mean, it's like sending the blind Chirrut Imwe in *Rogue One: A Star Wars Story* into a fight against an entire battalion of stormtroopers. He might manage to flip the switch and not get hit by a blaster, but he'll still die from the explosion.

"We're handling energy. We're harvesting it from the space around us and using those 'dance moves' you speak of to manipulate the energy."

"I can see that, but how does positive energy combat an eyeball that can turn you to stone?"

The wizard narrows his gaze at me. "And why is it that you're worried about the monster who turns people to stone?"

"I assumed you already knew the reason. Aren't you the all-knowing, the all-powerful wizard?"

Scott shifts uncomfortably. He's wondering if I'm antagonizing the wizard too much and if he'll need to fight him to protect me, or if he should just let him smack me around a little bit to knock some sense into me.

Gallean waves for me to join them. "I see that you and I are going to need several contemplative conversations together. It takes you a long time to trust another—as it does me. And as yet, I don't trust you."

It's the first time anybody has ever voiced their distrust of me out loud. I mean, sure plenty of teachers didn't trust me. That's why they hid the scissors and staplers. The principal didn't trust me either, because every time he had given me a free pass, I proved to him that he shouldn't have. I came to embrace the distrust of those in authority in Vernal Falls, but my friends and family always trusted me. I lied, I cheated, I stole, and they trusted me in spite of that. And now here's this man, this all-knowing wizard who doesn't trust me even though he knows I'm a reincarnated goddess.

Scott goes on guard. He figures I'll either go after Gallean or hurt myself. But he needn't worry. Rather than being pissed off and annoyed with Gallean's attitude, I'm actually starting to like the old guy.

"Can you show me how to do that?"

Scott gives me a smug smile as if to say, "I told you so." I roll my eyes at him and begin to fall into the rhythms the wizard's modeling for us.

I lift my outstretched hands facing palm up toward my chest. I can actually feel energy form into a ball. I push the energy ball out in front of me, almost releasing it. Before it fully escapes, I pull it back into my chest and push it down. My hands move up and down in the rhythm of the flow Gallean and Scott are in. I'll never admit it to them, but I feel the energy coursing through the air. I've always felt it, but I've never used it.

"By using the energy around you, you are able to maintain your own strength," Gallean says as if reading my mind.

Great, another one of them.

"When you use your own energy—as you have a tendency to do, Gigi—you wind up depleted. If your enemy were able to withstand you for a short burst of time, they would soon find they could get the upper hand and, in your case, kill your earthly form and rid the world of a god forever."

I try to swallow the lump in my throat. I've thought about my own mortality before, but I've never really considered the impact my death would have on the world. Gram, Dad, Granda, Clarissa, they all told me what would happen, but I didn't believe them. It took Gallean to make it real for me.

The thought of Brigit, a goddess who cares about her people more than anything, no longer existing is a fate the world should never experience. I will not do that to them.

"Would I be able to use this energy in a fight? At the bonfire on Samhain, I couldn't do anything. I watched my father get attacked and Scott tortured, and all I could do was stand there like a fucking asshole."

"You were able to do something."

I remember the shield I dropped over myself, then Scott, and how I could stretch it to include others. "Yes, but what good is a shield?"

"As soon as someone entered the shield, they were protected. You were able to protect them and keep them from harm. You could stretch and manipulate the shield. You can throw it out in front of you or to the side or behind you."

"But—"

"But that takes energy, and you can either deplete your own or harvest the energy around you."

"I guess it's harvest time then."

For the next few hours we practice our dance routine. In the beginning I was clumsy, and awkward, and freaking uncomfortable. I felt like I was thirteen all over again, but at least those were emotions I was well familiar with. Once I was able to manipulate and push and pull that energy, it was like the skies opened and a giant beam of light shined down upon me. It soon became a natural movement, and I could feel the power of energy generating around me and within me and the way it felt to pull and push it. Best natural high ever.

I juggle an energy ball back and forth in my hands. "Can I shoot one of these at someone?"

Scott continues to manipulate his. "Leave it to Gigi to think about violent ends."

"Easy for you to say, Scott. Your power wasn't hampered when we were fighting."

His shoulders slump. "But I wasn't able to draw on my power then."

Gallean keeps moving even though Scott and I have both stopped. "When were you able to use it?"

Scott glances at me. "It wasn't until the power swirled around me in a tornado and Gigi admitted that she was in love with Clayone's son that I was able to control it."

Gallean pulls a large energy ball back into this chest. "There are many lessons, and they occur when they are meant to. It is important to take advantage of the lessons when they arrive. Do not regret the past. Look forward to the future."

The emotional level lies heavy on us, and I take it upon myself to bring some humor to the situation. "Gallean, I didn't know you also wrote greeting cards for Hallmark."

He pushes the energy back into the ground. "Again, I don't understand your references, Gigi. Scott, there is no point lamenting on the limits of the past. It only holds bad energy. It'll only hamper your progress for the future."

Scott returns to pulling and pushing the energy. He's really taking the training seriously. I guess I am too. As I crack my neck from side to side, preparing for my next round of energy work, something catches my attention at the end of the tunnel. I move to look more closely and sense the energy mass from yesterday.

With Gallean's training and my increased awareness of the energy particles around me, it's clearer. I concentrate and try to read the mind of whoever might be hiding in the shadows.

Gallean steps in front of me. "Shall we continue with our afternoon activities?"

If he thinks he can distract me after I've had a full night's sleep, he is mistaken. "Is someone standing there?"

He shifts uncomfortably, still blocking my line of sight.

I move to get a better angle, but his giant body keeps getting in the way. "Who are you hiding?"

"No one."

Scott's mind fills with an incredible need to discover who it is. He heads for the tunnel, but not at regular human speed. He moves at super-fast god speed.

"Don't!" Gallean yells as Scott nears the end of the tunnel. "It is not time for you to meet."

We both stop and look at the wizard. "Meet? Who are we meeting?"

I stare down the tunnel again, trying to form a body out of the energy particles. Whoever was there has disappeared.

Scott senses as much too, and suddenly appears next to me at his super-fast god speed. Of course he gets blessed with increased athletic prowess, and I can almost read shadow minds—big fecking deal.

"How was this person able to penetrate your protection boundaries, Gallean?" he says.

"That is not your concern."

He stands in front of the wizard. "I disagree. It is our concern. There are monsters ready to kill us. I believe we have the right to know how this person was able to penetrate your protective barriers and observe our training. How do you know this person is not an enemy? Or somebody who will pretend to be your ally and then turn against you?"

Scott has never questioned a person's truth before. It's always been that way. But now I see him for who he really is —the powerful God of Love filled with passion.

Gallean straightens to his full height. As tall as he is, he is nothing compared to the god before him. "Who are you to question me? You arrive at my keep. I agree to train you, and this is the gratitude I receive? Be gone today. Be gone from my sight."

Well, that's an unexpected turn of events. Scott wanted nothing more than to get to the Shadow Realm and learn to control his magic from Gallean, and now Gallean wants to kick us out?

If the wizard was hoping to defuse Scott's tension, he made a grave logistical error. "You refuse to train us?"

Gallean stands as a formidable opponent even without tapping into his magic. Scott's not backing down and neither is he. Powerful energy swirls in the air. I sense Gallean harnessing the energy around him, but Scott uses his own. Soon a tornado forms above his head.

I remember Gallean's lesson from earlier, about how if I were to use my own energy and an opponent was able to withstand it, they could defeat me once I was depleted. Looks like my brother needs a refresher.

"Scott, you must control it. Don't use your own energy."

He has so many thoughts whirling around his brain I can't get a read on him. All I know is that he refuses to be swayed.

"Scott, you can't win this. What are you doing?"

"There's something he's not telling us. Something really important. That shadow belongs to somebody important to us. Important to me."

Gallean's stoic face reveals not even a hint of emotion. "And I told you, you're not ready to meet yet."

His response infuriates Scott. The tornado builds. It

sounds like a freaking freight truck is barreling down at us. "Who are you to decide? Who are you to tell us who we can meet and when?"

My brother unravels before my eyes. He keeps tapping into his own energy and his well is quickly depleting.

Gallean appraises his demeanor. "You are unable to use magic here. Gigi is also unable to use magic here."

This was news to me. "Then why are we here if not to use our magic?"

"You were sent here to learn to use the energy around you. You will learn how to manipulate the energy, but not your magic."

Gallean called Scott "the Angry One" the very first time we met in the seomra de rúin. I didn't see it before, but I see it now. If it comes to a fight, it won't end well for either one of us.

15

SEVEN OF SWORDS

*C*aer hadn't slept again last night. The betrayal she'd felt at the hands of the wizard proved too painful to do much else than curl up in a tight ball, slice open her soul, and let it pour out onto the cave floor. The final insult had come when he wouldn't allow her inside the courtyard to watch because the sister could see her too.

Was the sister as powerful as the wizard? The question kept plaguing her. It was doubtful. She was too young to have possessed mastery of skills that had taken the wizard decades, maybe even centuries to learn.

Caer wished her assassination attempt hadn't been interrupted by the wizard. If she had succeeded, it would have been her in his courtyard today training with real blades and swords rather than pushing and pulling energy around like the brother and sister.

After much internal debate and an almost insurmountable amount of conflict. Caer knew she couldn't stay away from Gallean's keep. She'd heed his warning and observe them from outside the tunnel. Even from a distance, she could still learn from him. As he'd said, she had acquired most of her skills that way anyway.

She held her shame close to her. The tantrum she had thrown in front of the wizard after he refused to continue training her embarrassed her. The wizard didn't comprehend that, for Caer, everything had changed once he finally acknowledged her presence. Finally someone else knew of her existence aside from Balor. Someone else knew her story.

She still didn't understand why he wouldn't allow her to meet the brother and sister. He spoke of their trio of power and not being able to control it. If the most powerful wizard couldn't control it, how would three untrained individuals be able to when they finally met?

She stepped cautiously through the first barrier. She felt her invisibility waiver, but it stayed in place. The three barriers kept out everyone with the exception of Caer, and now, the brother and sister. If the three of them could pass through, who else could? It was a question she'd need to ask Gallean if she could get him alone.

After each barrier, she checked to ensure her invisibility was intact. At the final one, she slid over to the outside wall of the keep and peeked down the tunnel. The three danced in the same courtyard she and Gallean had trained in for hand-to-hand combat the day before. Frustration reblossomed within her. The dance wouldn't teach her how to fight Balor. If she mimicked the wizard's movements, she didn't know if she could adopt them into battle formation. She wouldn't know until she was in the thick of it. She'd watch and learn from him for now because it was her only recourse.

After only a few hours of practice the brother and sister sat and ate again. They spent more time stuffing their faces and wagging their tongues than training. Each day that she had practiced with Gallean, they had eaten breakfast and then hadn't stopped training until evening. She was glad they hadn't wasted time eating when she'd had so many lessons to learn. Thank the gods too, because the brother and sister ended her training.

They were of a weaker constitution than Caer. Gallean took pity on them. He did not pity her. She didn't need his pity. Pity implied weakness, and Caer knew weakness would only get her killed.

After their break she studied the sister. What made her more worthy of Gallean's attention than Caer? They'd only been at it for a few minutes and already sweat beaded on her brow. She shouldn't be fatigued so soon. She'd never last in a real battle.

Suddenly the sister's spine stiffened. She spun around and stared at her. Caer swallowed. She couldn't possibly see her, and there was no reason she'd suspect someone was watching them. The brother followed his sister's gaze and began heading in her direction. Before Caer could think, he was almost upon her, moving faster than any human she'd ever seen.

Gallean yelled at the brother to stop.

Go, he roared in Caer's head so loudly she threw her hands to her ears, thinking her head would explode.

Go, he shouted again, but she couldn't. She felt immobilized, just like the night before, except now it wasn't Gallean casting his energy upon her, it was the brother. It was not a magical energy, though. Something about him gave her pause. Even now as he approached what he believed to be an uninvited guest, his green eyes sparkled with mischief.

Gallean yelled at the brother again. He glanced over his shoulder at the wizard. It was enough to break his spell over Caer, and she fled.

Do not return, Gallean warned her.

Tears welled at the corners of her eyes. After spending less than a day with the brother and sister, the wizard no longer wanted her near. He'd discarded her like yesterday's pheasant carcass.

As she ran from the keep, she loathed the thought of spending the rest of her life alone. The village was just a short distance from Gallean's. She'd go there and find someone who did want her.

Standing on the hill, she watched the smoke spiral from some of the huts in the village. Her heart pounded as she wondered what it must be like to stroll freely through the streets. She had walked through them many times before, but always under the cloak of darkness and her invisibility. Today she planned to shed her gift and interact with people. They'd see her for what she was—a young woman in need of companionship. Balor's spies, if there were any, would never suspect she was the trophy their master sought.

She took a deep breath and shed the invisibility around her. Before she could change her mind, she quickly climbed down the slope and entered the closest pub, one with a howling wolf engraved on a sign above the door. A few patrons glanced in her direction as she entered. They looked her up and down, taking in her sword and armor. She worried she'd made a mistake, but they soon decided she was not a threat and returned to their tankards. She stepped farther into the room. One man, younger than the others, kept watching her. Something about the yearning in his eyes made her itch with discomfort. She wished she could cloak herself with her invisibility, but it was too late for that.

She steadied herself and approached the bar. She had no

coin and nothing to barter with other than her sword and knife, and she'd part with neither.

Behind the bar a woman with cleavage to spare eyed Caer. Caer shifted uncomfortably, but she wouldn't hide anymore. She'd spent a lifetime in the shadows. It was time to be warmed by the sun. Soon the woman asked her, "What will it be?"

Caer studied the shelf behind the bar. There were dusty bottles of all shapes and sizes. Once, when she'd had an injured toe, she had stolen one of the brown bottles to pour over her foot to stave off infection. Mathair Mhór had taught her to use what was available. The Land of Shadows had different seasons than her former lands, so certain healing herbs were not attainable. Luckily, fermented beverages were always in abundant supply.

"Buy you a drink?" a man's hard voice asked as he grabbed her arm.

Caer's fingers longed to unsheathe her sword, but she didn't reach for it. The man was the reason she had entered The Howling Wolf. She glanced at the man whose fingers encircled her arm and saw it was the one who had watched her enter. He'd do for what she had in mind. She nodded at him. Words were unnecessary when gestures would do.

"Two drinks," he said throwing up two of his fingers at the barmaid.

As the drinks were poured, he turned to Caer. "What brings you to these parts?"

"You," she breathed just above a whisper.

He raised an eyebrow in surprise. His black eyes were flat and lifeless, possessing none of the spark of the brother's.

Scott, a voice whispered in her mind. *His name is Scott.*

Caer blocked the brother's name from her thoughts. It would only make what she wanted to do more difficult.

"Do you want to drink, or do you want to get out of here?" he asked, reaching for her waist.

She gauged this man. A thick beard covered most of his face, and his heavy clothing hid his true size and stature. She guessed he was muscular, but nothing compared to the brother. She could take him in a fight if it came down to it, but she didn't plan to stick around long enough after they were done to find out.

He leaned into her. "Let's get out of here."

He led her outside and turned a corner to the side of The Howling Wolf. It was daylight, but the narrow alleyway was empty. He pushed her up against the building. Definitely not gently, but not entirely rough either. He leaned in with his mouth open. He smelled of sour ale and sweat. Though she'd never been kissed before, she tried not to cringe as his tongue waggled against hers. None of it was how she imagined it to be.

The brother's face appeared before her, unbidden. She tried to close her mind to him and immerse herself in the man's embrace instead. Where the brother's strong lips promised her pleasure, the man's weak upper lip brought nothing but disgust. His teeth banged against hers again and again as he searched her mouth for . . . well, she didn't know what.

Eventually she pulled her face away from him, but he didn't seem to mind. He found her neck instead, licking and sucking in a manner that reminded her of a slug. He reached under her armor and fondled her breasts. His rough hands grabbed and pinched her. She knew some women might find his efforts stimulating, but she wanted nothing more than to shove a knife in his neck.

When his hand crawled down between her legs, the face of the brother appeared again. She knocked the man's hand away.

"You'll do best if you don't resist me," he growled, trying to shove his hand inside her leggings.

This time she twisted her body as she knocked his hand away again.

"You be nothing but a tease."

Her fingers itched again. She knew it had nothing to do with anything the man was trying to do to her. She had wanted to lie with him, but now, in the moment, it was the last thing she wanted. He gripped her waist with one arm as he unbuckled his pants with his other. He planned to force himself into her.

That wasn't going to happen.

She reached over her head and yanked the sword from her scabbard. She forced him away with a mighty kick and held the sword between them.

His gaze trailed the length of the blade to the ruby-studded handle. "That's not a sword from around here." His eyes gleamed. "I'll take that from you," he said, reaching for the handle.

"It'll be the last thing you take," she warned, low and deep.

Without thinking, she sliced his throat. Blood spurted out between his fingers as he clutched the wound. He screamed, stumbling away from her and into the street, collapsing just as he rounded the corner. Soon shouts and warnings echoed through the village. Her time in the company of others had come to an end. Too many people had seen her already. Rumors would spread, just as they had when she went swimming with the children. Balor would find her, even in the Land of Shadows. She pulled her invisibility around her and escaped down the rear of the alley.

Adrenaline coursed through her as she ran from the village. She couldn't return to Gallean's keep. He didn't want her anyway. But the high of killing the man filled her with confidence. If she could find Balor's weak spot, she could kill him just as she had the man. In order to do so, she needed to go to the very place he'd least expect her.

A shimmering light appeared before her. Without hesitation, she stepped through it.

It was time to go home.

16

DREAM THIEVES

*G*allean grins at me. It's the first emotion he's displayed during this testosterone-induced battle. Well, Scott's testosterone-induced battle. "Now, do you understand why I call him the Angry One?"

I glance at my wigged-out brother, then back at Gallean, finally realizing why Scott's so upset, though I don't think he even knows why. "It's her, isn't it."

Gallean doesn't answer, but I know I'm right. The Shadow Girl is Scott's swan.

"We need to diffuse his energy," Gallean says. "He should not have been able to tap into his own reserves so deeply here."

Scott's oblivious to our conversation. He wants to beat the truth out of Gallean but recognizes that he probably shouldn't do that. The storm intensifies above him as he rounds the courtyard.

"Do you have any ideas? You egged him on."

The wizard studies the tornado over Scott's head. "I may have gone too far."

"You think?" I snap at him.

"It is fascinating. I've never seen anything like it."

Remembering the damage Scott caused back at Granda's cottage, I'm definitely not a fan of Scott the my-own-personal-tornado god. "Trust me, once you've seen one, you don't want to witness another."

"How does he harness it? Or does he send it out?"

Gallean and I watch him circle the courtyard at superhuman speed. After about the seventh time around, the tornado begins to subside. Around the twenty-first, the tornado drifts back into him and he circles back around to us.

He knows he acted like a freaking moron. He worries that if Gallean refuses to train him, he'll hurt everyone he cares about along with innocent people. "Do we really need to leave?"

Gallean studies him for several long moments. Scott shrinks under the wizard's scrutiny. Finally Gallean says, "You do not."

Scott exhales loudly. "Thank the gods."

"Don't thank them. It was I who allowed you to remain. Now, let's continue."

Scott dips his head as he turns to me. His cheeks burn with embarrassment. "Sorry about that whole thing."

"You don't need to apologize. No harm, no 'fowl'—although I do miss your feathered friends."

He rolls his eyes. "I suppose I deserve that one."

I stand on my tiptoes and pretend to scrutinize the top of his shirt, though I'd need twelve-inch heels to actually see it. "Look on the bright side. At least you don't have bird shit on your shoulders."

"No, I don't," he says with a twinge of sadness. He doesn't fully understand why he became so angry at Gallean. He suspects the wizard is keeping secrets from him, but for the time being, he'll keep his suspicions to himself or run the risk of getting kicked out again. He doesn't realize that it was his swan at the end of the tunnel. He doesn't know who it was, just that the person was important to him. I want to tell him his swan is in the Shadow Realm, but Gallean wants to keep that juicy tidbit from him until the timing is right.

The trouble is, Gallean doesn't fully appreciate how masterfully skilled Scott and I are at screwing up even universally aligned, meteorologically coordinated events. Releasing Clayone was proof of that godly power. Our early arrival to the Shadow Realm, another. It doesn't matter how planned out our meeting could be, Scott and Gigi—mostly Gigi—will figure out a way to screw it up.

Surprisingly, we lasted two more days without any tornado episodes on Scott's part, and I haven't managed to partake in any serious mayhem, which is kind of a shame. But let me tell you, my body freaking aches. I have pains and bruises on muscles I didn't know existed. For twelve hours a day, Gallean puts us through rigorous rounds of his dance routine. I used to think that my old gym classes were torture. At least I could skip those. Here, if I try to avoid a session, Gallean finds me. He drags me out of bed. He pulls me back from beyond his borders when I pretend I'm searching for a particular herb. He even found me when I climbed onto to the roof of the keep. I suspect he might have some sort of energy-tracking spell on me. If I knew how to remove it I would, but our magic doesn't work in this realm.

I still don't understand why Granda and Clarissa thought Gallean was the only one who could teach us to use our magic if we can't even use it here. I mean, sure, I've learned how to push and pull the energy around me and how to harvest it for my own use but what happens when a psycho-witch comes after me? Will I be able to handle her in a magic duel?

As if the aches and pains aren't bad enough, I barely sleep, even though I'm completely exhausted. And when I finally do crash, the nightmares come. They began with Lizzie chaining Alaric to a table. Every time he called my name, even in a whisper, she'd turn a handle and he'd scream in pain. At first his calls to me increased. Not because he wanted me to save him. It was more that he longed for me, just as I longed for him. Then, over the course of the nightmares, as Lizzie tortured him at every utterance of my name, he eventually stopped. It was his silence that scared me the most.

When had Lizzie become so twisted? Was it when she changed into a werewolf?

But werewolves could be capable of good. Alaric's good—he'd never dream of hurting me. And Madigan's good—he's helping us find Alaric. How did Lizzie get all twisted?

I showed her the spell book.

Twist.

She stole the spell book from me.

Twist.

She tried to curse Kensey in the hall.

Twist.

She bought the eyeball necklace.

Twist.

Carman took possession of her.

Twist.

She tortured Kensey in the attic.

Twist. Twist.

It was her idea to go camping—Ryan admitted that to us after she died.

Twist.

She was bitten by Clayone.

Twist. Twist.

She died and later became a werewolf.

Twist.

And then the most startling realization . . .

Clayone created her.

Twist. Twist. Twisted.

Scott isn't faring much better than I am. The bags under his eyes make him a candidate for old people eye cream, and each day they get worse. I try not to stare. I don't want to pry. I get it. My nightmares about Lizzie turning Alaric against me are enough to drive any god mad.

By now, even his dance moves have become affected. Scott is supposed to be the jock of the family. He's the one blessed with athletic prowess. He's blessed with the brains too, though I'd never tell him that.

At this point, he can't even try to eat the eggs and fruit that Gallean prepared for us. He just pushes the food around on his plate.

I sit beside him. "What's bothering you, Scott?"

"Nothing," he sighs.

"Well, something's bothering you."

He looks over at me his green eyes serious. "Do you believe in dreams?"

A pit forms in my stomach. If I believed in the dreams I'd been having, I'd never sleep again. The possibility that my werewolf best friend is torturing Alaric into hating me? I can't believe it.

"I guess the question is not whether I believe in my dreams but whether you believe in yours?"

Wow, I really sound philosophically advanced.

"I don't know what you've been dreaming," he says. "We've barely talked since we got here."

"Gallean doesn't leave much time for conversation. I actually think he's trying to kill us through a long, torturous death with pirouettes and downward dogs."

"You wouldn't be so lucky," Gallean says, sitting down to join us. "Now, what is this about dreams and believing in them?"

Scott swallows. He doesn't want to share his dreams with Gallean. He doesn't really want to share them with me either, but they're doing something to him. I didn't think dreams could break someone, but Scott is proof that maybe they can.

"Go on," Gallean says. "Don't be afraid to share. In order to attain your full potential as Oegden, you must acknowledge all of your truths."

"It's just . . ." he starts. "I don't . . ." he tries. "I . . ."

I rest my hand on him. "Scott," I whisper, "it's okay."

"I keep dreaming of this . . . of this girl."

"And it's affecting your sleep?" Gallean asks.

"Yes . . . and no. It's like . . ." he tries again. "I've never . . . I just want to keep sleeping in order to be with her. It's like I don't want to wake up in the morning, and I can't wait to go to bed at night."

Gallean leans in, curiosity coloring his features. "Has she come every night since you've been here?"

"Not the first night, but each night since. She's all I can think about."

I squeeze his hand. "Who is she?"

"I don't know. Someone I've never met before, but it's like . . . I've always known her. Does that make sense?"

I'm not thrilled about pouring my guts out to Gallean, but I will for Scott. If I can make him feel even a smidge better, I will. "It does. I feel the same way about Alaric. Even when I found out who his father was and the potential danger I could be in, it didn't matter. I know him."

"I want to find her. I feel like she's . . ." he searches for the right phrasing, "I feel like she's so lonely, and all I want to do is comfort her. Make her realize that she's not alone."

I leap up and hold out my hand to him. "Where do we start?"

He looks up at me. "You'd help me find her?"

"Of course. You're my brother."

"But Alaric is still missing."

And that's when I decide it's time to share with Scott a little about Gallean's visitor. "Yes, but we're here in the Shadow Realm. Maybe she is too."

Well done, Gallean places in my head, then turns to Scott. "Can you describe the place where she is?"

"It's a large lake. A really large lake."

"Think harder," he demands.

Scott closes his eyes and looks within himself for an answer that makes sense, that would give us some indication of where this mystery girl could be. Finally, he opens them. "At the head of the dragon. Does that make any sense?"

Gallean rests his forefingers against the edge of his chin. "She's returned then," he says barely above a whisper.

I whip my head around. "You do know her. Why didn't you say something?"

"It is not for me to share with you your past, your present, or your future. I am just a guide along the way, teaching you the means with which to utilize your power."

Scott is far from satisfied with Gallean's answer. He aches deeply for someone he doesn't even know. "You have to tell me more. You have to tell me how to find her."

"She'll come to you when she's ready."

I cross my arms over my chest. "I hate waiting."

Gallean stands up from the table and Scott follows him over to the courtyard. "The best thing you can do is train."

I follow behind them. "That's awfully convenient, don't you think?"

He stops and looks at me, puzzled. "How do you mean?"

"You know who this 'mystery' person is"—I even use air quotes—"and you know where she is, and yet, you are unwilling to help Scott find her or tell him her name."

Scott had already returned to the pull and push rhythm of Gallean's dance, but he stops when he realizes what I've said to Gallean. "That's who was here when we arrived. That's who you were talking to. You kept me from her. The next day it was her outside the keep. That's why you tried to send us away."

Gallean begins to push and pull the energy. "Everything happens in time. I will not have three gods, who are woefully naive of their powers, mucking everything up because they reincarnated as impatient teenagers rather than thoughtful, contemplative gods."

So Scott's swan is a goddess. That's news to me. I don't remember Granda or Clarissa mentioning anything about her being a goddess.

"That's not for you to decide," Scott says. "You do not possess the power to make decisions for us. I need to know who she is."

"In time you will."

"I need to know now."

"You need to train now."

Scott glares at Gallean. He's pissed. And annoyed. And exhausted. He wants to keep arguing with the wizard, but it's far less satisfying than our fights. He'd get more information from one of the trees in the courtyard.

Rather than freaking out and allowing another natural disaster to erupt, he falls back into the rhythm of the dance.

I do too.

Maybe the wizard actually does know what he's doing.

17

TWO OF WANDS

*P*erhaps she shouldn't have entered the portal, but it was too late to second guess herself or to turn back anyway. The portal disappeared as quickly as it had descended upon the valley in the Land of Shadows.

Caer knew where she was without even taking in her surroundings. Something about her "powers," as Gallean had called them, allowed her to create portals to other dimensions. It was the second time she had done so. The first time she barely remembered. She had just discovered that Mathair Mhór and Nimblefoot had perished in the fire set by Balor's men. One moment she'd been blinded with sadness and rage, hands wrapped tightly around her sword intending to attack his men. The next, she'd found herself in a foreign land, far from the smoldering remains of Mathair Mhór's hut.

She guessed that, this time, the disappointment she'd felt after Gallean kicked her out, along with the exhilaration at killing the brute who'd tried to take her against her will, were enough of an onslaught of emotions to generate a portal. But could she call one at will? She didn't know.

Out of a desire to test her skill, she concentrated on her

cave in the Land of Shadows. The very one to which her first portal had taken her. She tried to rekindle the emotions she'd felt that day long ago when the smoke had crept up her nose and woken her. She'd never forget the fear and the knowing that Mathair Mhór was in grave danger. She had raced down the mountain but was too late. Only ashes remained of the hut, along with the charred skeletons of Mathair Mhór and Nimblefoot.

Tears sprung to her eyes. She swiped them away. She had cried enough these past few days. Enemies would only think her weak if they knew she wept for an old woman and a scruffy pony who had died so many years before. She closed her eyes against the tears and the memories.

Her vision was blurred when she finally opened them, but it wasn't because of any portal. Her crying couldn't be helped, yet her emotions still weren't enough to warrant a portal. Or maybe it hadn't appeared because she needed to complete the task she had come here to do.

As she stood on the shoreline over the lake, she pulled her invisibility around her. She studied the opposite shore and the rough outline of a castle with peaks and towers as familiar to her as the woods surrounding Mathair Mhór's hut had once been.

In several of the windows, she could see the glow of a fireplace or candles glinting in the darkness. A light flickered in her old room. Had Balor taken up residency there in the hopes that the princess would eventually return? Or did he keep it lit, knowing that one day he'd catch his prize? Another light flickered in the window three floors above hers. Her father's room. Her heart quickened in an excited flourish, only to seize up when she realized it could never be her father. She had witnessed Balor slice his throat.

The memories, still fresh following her breakthrough with Gallean, came rushing back to her. If Balor had indeed

KB ANNE

taken her father's room, she'd find her way back into the tunnels and return the favor. For she didn't plan to leave this realm until one of them was dead.

The moon rose in the sky as she watched the castle for movement. Aside from a few servants, the castle appeared empty. Impatience plagued her. She wanted to test the castle's defenses and get inside. She didn't know how much time it would take Balor's sorcerer to discover she was there, so there was no time to delay. She easily climbed over the gate and hurried across the bridge to the main entrance, sticking to the shadows—a place she was very familiar with.

She peeked into the guards' entrance and saw him slumped over at a table, sound asleep. She suspected there weren't many who sought entrance to the castle now that Balor reigned, and she doubted enemies would dare use the guards' entrance as their passage into the castle. Once through, she entered into the servants' hallway.

All at once footsteps pounding on stone echoed down to her. Her heart raced at the prospect of being caught before she had even gotten started. She glanced wildly up and down the corridor. Though her invisibility ensured that she couldn't be seen, the narrow passage left little room for any to pass without knocking into her. She flung her body flat against the wall. Her hands clung to the cold stone as she tried to calm her breath. Soon, three men covered in leather armor with swords and bows on their backs approached.

"That was a fine piece of tail you took this evening," the one closest to her roared as he smacked the back of the man in the middle.

He grunted in reply.

"He's just lucky I didn't take her first," the farthest one said.

The three cackled as they shuffled down the hall, boasting about their evening's activities as they drew ever closer.

Caer doubted very much that they'd been sent to find her, but in their current drunken state they might just stumble upon her by accident.

Her nose tickled as they approached. They stank of sweat and rotten game. She pressed her body against the wall. Her fingers itched to draw her sword. She wanted nothing more than to end their lives, but their dead bodies would seal her fate.

The brute in the middle suddenly doubled over, clutching his stomach right in front of her. "Oi," he moaned.

"What's the matter? Can't hold your ale?" The farthest laughed, whacking him on the back.

He groaned.

"I bet the trollop cursed his pulling prick. Would serve him right too. She was mine," the one closest to her said, letting out a great guffaw while nearly tripping into her. She jerked to the right before he could make contact and stole down the hallway as quickly as her feet would take her. When she rounded the corner, she fell against the wall and sighed in relief. As the men's voices became more and more distant, she knew she was safe—at least temporarily.

When she recognized where she was, a smile crept to her lips. It was happenstance that she'd wound up exactly where she wanted to be. She glanced up and down the hallway to ensure she was alone before easing into her father's royal throne room.

His throne still sat upon the dais, high above where his loyal subjects would have stood. At one time his men had flanked the throne, but they'd provided no protection on the night of Samhain. The night of his death. She assumed they had been slaughtered along with her father.

The King, a kind and generous man, had never turned

away a guest seeking respite from the elements and an evening of entertainment. Bards praised his hospitality, and his power had grown with each enchanted tale. There were many who envied his position, but it was not until he allowed Balor, the giant one-eyed pirate, to enter the castle that his life was at risk.

She stared at the throne, imagining what it might be like to sit in it and rest her hands upon the intricately carved wood arms. Would she sense her father's presence after all these years? Had his blood sunk deep into the grain, becoming part of the throne that marked him as leader of the kingdom even after his death? And if she sat upon it, would she be their queen?

She dared not linger. Though Balor did not seem to be at the castle, she didn't want to risk getting caught. Her near encounter with his men left her shaken. She merely wanted to reacquaint herself with the hallways and hidden tunnels of the castle. The element of surprise was crucial if she wished to be successful when she attacked Balor at his most vulnerable.

She slipped into the royal washroom hidden in the back corner of the throne room. All but the King were forbidden from entering. Caer had never managed to sneak into it as a child, but now she suspected the method with which she would kill Balor lay beyond the entrance of it.

The first indication that something was amiss should have come when she saw the carving of the reptile on the door as she pushed into the stone, but she didn't hesitate. Hesitation indicated weakness, and the mere suggestion of weakness while in Balor's realm would mean her death. Or worse—her capture.

The stone floor of the washroom sloped downward to a spring that carried the royal waste far away from its source. A wooden stall enclosed what must house the royal privy. It was strange that the King would have a private stall within a washroom forbidden to everyone else, but she had never fully understood certain rules of the castle.

She pushed open the door and knew at once that it was a mistake. A figure, her head covered with coiled snakes, rose to meet her. Sensing Caer's presence, the snakes began to writhe and hiss. Caer shut her eyes and jumped backward, slamming the door closed. Her heart raced as she remembered teachings from Mathair Mhór of an ancient goddess whose head was covered with snakes and who could turn people to stone. She didn't remember what had become of the goddess, but perhaps she'd just found out.

Caer backed away from the stall. Her curiosity had almost gotten her killed. She'd have to be careful not to make the same mistake again.

Sometime between entering the stall and the snakes coming to life, the floor had shifted from stone to packed dirt. She turned to leave, sensing that the royal washroom was far more magical than it ought to be. A low snarl to her right caught her off guard. She twisted her body, her blade already in hand, ready to kill the beast who saw fit to attack her.

Dozens of sharp teeth flashed before her, clamping down on her leg.

She screamed, leaping away from the giant crocodile before it could take her entire leg with it. Its teeth had already managed to rip off a chunk of her calf.

"Owwww! You bastard!" she hissed through clenched teeth. The reptile replied by lunging again. This time Caer was ready. She swung her sword, slicing the beast's head off as she jumped to the far side of the spring. She'd gained the upper ground without even planning on it. Good thing, too, because the washroom had transformed into a croc den in the midst of her fight. If she had remained on the side with the dead croc, she would have become dinner to an army of them.

She assessed her surroundings as the wizard had taught her during their short time together. She didn't like what she saw. At least fifty feet of croc-infested royal washroom blocked her from even considering the door back to the throne room as her escape.

She quickly glanced down the spring's dark tunnel, hoping to see a glimmer of light peeking back at the end of it. Her wish was short-lived. There was nothing but darkness. And the wall closest to her was impenetrable rock. It appeared that an early descendant had situated the royal privy at the source of the spring. The sewer tunnel was her only option.

Teeth gnashed against each other as the crocs advanced toward her. Jaws opened and closed, anticipating their next meal, but it was the rush of water that drew her attention back to the spring. What was once a slow trickle was quickly becoming a channel. She'd have to hurry or her only chance of safety would be cut off.

She drew in a breath and jumped before she could over-think her escape route. Water splashed around her as she landed in the now ankle-deep spring. She sprinted down the tunnel, running as if her life depended on it, which it did. Her calf throbbed where the croc had bitten her, but with the water now past her knees, she couldn't stop and bandage it. Soon the crocs would be able to swim after her and finish what their dead comrade had started.

Caer sloshed down the tunnel, hanging onto the hope that the blackness swallowing her would make it more diffi-cult for the crocs to find her. Although they could probably follow the scent of blood flowing from her leg, she wanted to remain hopeful.

She gripped her sword, ready for whatever beast might

jump out ahead of her. She had only her sense of hearing to alert her to the dangers surrounding her.

The handle of the sword tingled in her palm and the sensation crept up her arm. She almost dropped the blade in surprise. After so many years in the Land of Shadows, she wasn't used to the explosion of magic occurring in this realm.

The tingling became almost too painful to touch, but she dared not let the sword go. Soon a soft blue light began to emanate from the blade. The rough, hand-carved walls of the tunnel took shape around her as the light grew.

Now that she could see where she was going, she splashed through the water with greater speed. It was already to her thighs. Her muscles burned with the strain of moving through the high water, but her long hours of training had prepared them for this assault.

A loud splash echoed through the tunnel from behind. She was out of time. A huge wave knocked her forward, throwing her neck-deep into the water. The sword continued to glow from beneath the depths. Surge after surge smashed against her, trying to push her underwater. She fought to keep her head above it, but with the water level now almost to the ceiling, she soon had no choice but to swim.

A final surge knocked her off her feet and tossed her under the water. Her body jerked back and forth. Sensations shot down her arms and legs. Even her face twinged and pinched. Pain rocketed through her. Gripping her blade to her chest, she tried to swim, but her body refused to obey. Her vision blurred and shifted. The blade slid out from her hand and wrapped around her neck, changing into a silver necklace. Her face elongated into something beak-like. Her arms and legs folded into her body, and suddenly she was no longer getting knocked into the walls of the tunnel. She was swimming. What once were her boots were now webbed feet, jettisoning her through the tunnel.

The gnash and snap of crocodile teeth grew distant behind her. Whatever she had shifted into swam faster than a crocodile. Caer hadn't even made the decision to swim. Her body had made it for her.

The walls of the tunnel closed in around her. She torpedoed through them in this new form. If she hadn't shifted, she would never have made it through. She doubted the crocodiles would make it either.

The water dropped in temperature. Soon she blasted out of the tunnel into inky black open water. Her head—well, her beak—led her to the surface. She burst out of the water and flew through the air before landing gracefully on the surface of the lake. She released a sigh of relief at the faint outline of the castle. She had avoided capture once again.

She paddled over to the shoreline. It was then that the full impact of what happened hit her. Her arms, now wings, were covered with white feathers along with the rest of her body.

"What did I change into? What am I?"

But the only response she received was the squawking of a large flock of swans that soon surrounded her.

And, by the way they bowed their heads, she suspected she was their queen.

18

FLOWN THE COOP

*I*t's the middle of the night. My body craves sleep, but it is the last thing I want to do. I'm too terrified to cave in and close my eyes. The nightmares are getting worse. Alaric doesn't cry out for me anymore. Instead, whenever Lizzie mentions my name to him, his lip curls into a snarl. My dreams have always had a layer of truth in every single of one of them, so the whole snarling lip thing doesn't bode well for me. Unless, of course, Alaric is Elvis reincarnated. If the worst thing that could happen to us was getting all shook up, we'd be in great shape.

My crystal pendant from Clarissa warms against my chest along with the nightlock-imbued crystal. I added one the day Scott, Madigan, and I left to search for Alaric in the cavern. The day Scott and I fell through the portal. Thank goodness too, because if Alaric and I meet under a full moon, I don't want my throat to tempt him. I didn't grab a second one for Lizzie—I regret that decision now—but if there is any truth to my dreams, she might be beyond my reach.

The floor creaks outside my door. I jump out of bed.

Gallean's three layers of protection barriers are impenetrable, except, of course, if one is a reincarnated god, but maybe full gods can pass through them too. I pray to the other gods that Breas isn't prowling outside my door. I am not in the mood to deal with him.

I creep over, planning to use the element of surprise on my stalker. The plan would have worked too, if the alleged stalker hadn't opened the door and stuck his head in.

"Scott, what are you doing?" I hiss at him. These are the times I wished I carried around a foam noodle, so I could whack him in the head for scaring me.

"I can't sleep," he says. "Can I come in?"

"Sure," I reply more cheerfully than warranted because, hello, spending the entire night listening to Scott unload his issues outweighs the alternative of actually sleeping by at least fifty million.

"You couldn't sleep either?" he whispers as he makes himself comfortable on the corner of my bed.

I prop my pillow up and slip back under the covers. "No."

"Why not?" He genuinely wants to know. He'd also like a distraction from his own haunted mind, but no such luck from me. Unpacking my shit, even in whispers, will make it real, and my nightmares are freaky enough.

"Let's not go there. Let's wade through your crap tonight."

My ability to read his mind allows him to go right for the jugular.

"She comes to me when I sleep."

I know exactly who he's talking about. "That's good, right?"

"At first it was, but you've seen how the truth is gnawing away at me. This waiting for her . . . I hate it. If I don't meet her soon, I might do something I'll regret." He envisions Hurricane Maria hitting Puerto Rico then multiplies it by ten. We were only kids, but those images will stay with us for the rest of our lives. If Scott's capable of exacting more damage than that, we are fecked.

"But you haven't come close to that since our second day here."

"I keep it locked inside. I need Gallean to train me, but it's hard. I can't tell you how many times I almost blew it."

I had no idea he was struggling so much. But then, I was too busy getting my ass kicked by Gallean's dance moves to worry about Scott. I was just trying to survive. "You're good at hiding it."

He rakes his hands through his hair. "I'm tired of hiding it. I just want to find her. I wish I knew her name."

"I call her Shadow Girl."

He raises an eyebrow. "Shadow Girl?"

"Yeah, she hid in the shadows the whole time she was here. The name fits."

"Shadow Girl sounds exotic."

"Do you know what she looks like?"

An image of a gorgeous female pops into my head. Leather armor. A sword attached to her back. Leather pants. A lean body with mile-long legs. Black hair with white tufts. Of course, we need to discuss the hair situation, but first, my initial reaction: "She would totally kick your ass."

He gives me a knowing smile. "Yeah, she would."

"When did she come to you as a fully formed person?" Up until the other day he had only seen her spirit. It's her true being he's in love with. The exterior is just a bonus.

"Last night. And now I feel like there's a hole in my heart. I won't be content until I find her."

"Gallean doesn't want us to meet until it's time."

"When did you become a rule follower?"

"How dare you," I growl, karate kicking his leg.

"Ouch, that hurt."

"You're lucky I didn't have my boots on."

He rubs his leg. "What was that for?"

"For even suggesting I've changed into a rule follower. I was merely telling you what Gallean said, and that, clearly, we need to break out."

"I'm supposed to get that from a kick?"

I climb off the bed and grab my backpack from the table. "It would be much easier if you could read my mind, but alas, you have limitations. Now, grab your things and let's skip this joint."

He stands up beside me. "Do you think we should? What if we mess things up?"

I shake my head, laughing at him as I tug on my pants then my boots. "Of course we'll mess things up. Let's embrace that fact."

He considers my proposal for like a fraction of a second, then races out of the room.

Be right back.

He returns at his superhuman speed, completely dressed, with a backpack slung over his shoulder. "Ready?"

"Easy, speedy. Not everyone moves like Edward."

"Get over your vampire crush, and let's go."

I march over and punch him in the arm.

"What was that for?"

I show him my nightlock crystal. "Clearly, I'm Team Jacob."

"Right. Forgive me. Now let's go."

We creep down the hall. Scott slips into *Mission Impossible* spy mode. He glances back and forth, gives me the two-finger-to-eye-I-see-you move, then slips down the stairs. He's intentionally going slow so I can keep up. It's unfair that, even as a reincarnated goddess, I still lack any athletic prowess whatsoever, but Scott, who was already a freak-ishly athletic jock in his non-reincarnated god life is now full-on Captain America. I mean, couldn't I at least have gotten some of Wanda the Scarlet Witch's power so I can hurt the bad guys? But, nooooo, I'm a peace-loving goddess. Joy.

We hurry across the courtyard, being careful not to make a noise on the stones. Docs kick ass *and* no one hears them coming. After we pass through the tunnel, we break out in a run. We didn't plan it or make a big production, and say, "One, two, three, and run!" We just knew to get moving.

Scott keeps pace with me. I can tell he wants to carry me so we can go faster, but he knows I won't let him. I might not be speedy, but I am mighty. And proud. And really stubborn.

We approach the first barrier. Neither one of us thinks much of it, though we do notice that it's more visible in the darkness. We're five feet, four feet, three feet, then zap! We hit the barrier and get knocked backward, just like at Newgrange.

Scott stands back up. "Why can't we walk through it?"

I wave my hands along the edge of it. Now that I know the barrier at Newgrange not only keeps people out but also keeps people, magical creatures, and the like in, I suspect I know what's going on.

"You would be correct in your assumption," Gallean says, appearing next to us.

"Correct in what assumption?" Scott asks him.

"Gigi believes I'm trying to keep you here."

Scott swings his head back and forth between us. He thinks he should probably be mad, but he's also kind of relieved. "Are you?"

I'm already feeling claustrophobic, and to call me pissed would be a gross understatement. I wave my hand in front of the barrier. "Uh, hello? What does it look like to you? Yes, he's imprisoned us."

Scott crosses his arms. He won't try to get through the barrier, but he's not going back to the keep until he's satisfied. "Why, Gallean?"

"You need to be trained. Soon I will be unable to train you. You must learn."

He really knows how to work Scott, but his little speech won't persuade me. "You can't keep us prisoner."

Scott waves me off as if I'm a minor inconvenience. "Why won't you be able to train us? What will happen to you, Gallean?"

"It matters not. The universe prepares for the three of you, but the time has not yet come."

Gallean leads Scott back to the keep. I reluctantly follow. What else can I do?

Well, I could create a portal . . . like the one that got us here in the first place. I picture Granda's cottage and finding Alaric, and we're together by Brigit's sacred well, and—

"A portal won't work here," Gallean calls out to me.

"You don't know what I'm capable of," I mumble under my breath, still envisioning the sparkling water of the well.

"True, but I do know that while you're in my keep, you cannot create a portal."

I focus on Alaric—he's how we got here in the first place. I imagine pulling him into my arms and kissing him. I try to remember the way it feels when we're together and long for it.

"My keep suppresses all magic. Even that of reincarnated gods and goddesses."

"Not much fun in that."

"Perhaps not, but much safer."

Gigi, we need him.

I don't need him.

Maybe not, but I do.

You're pulling that card, are you?

Learned from the best.

Scott returns to me and reaches for my hand. "Together?"

I rest my hand in his and allow him to guide me. For Scott I will do anything.

19

THE WORLD

*C*aer now understood what her father had chanted when Balor had raised the blade to his throat. His last words weren't to save himself; they were to protect her. His sacrifice had turned her into this elegant beautiful creature who could swim, who could fly, who could escape from a monster.

The white tufts of hair marked her as Other. It's why Mathair Mhór had taken such trouble to hide them and forbade her from swimming or even bathing in the sunlight. All these years she had felt like a part of her was missing. Now she knew why.

Her body glided across the lake, feeling more natural than it ever had on land. True, compared to many she was gifted physically in human form. Her muscles were toned and shapely, capable of exacting murder or slipping coin out of a pocket. She was especially skilled with a sword and bow. Of course, her ability to go invisible lent itself to an array of capabilities she couldn't begin to count and made her weapon skills often unnecessary, though good to have. But being able to shift into a swan? That was a gift of love and a promise that, as a swan, she'd never be in need of company.

One hundred fifty swans served as her loyal subjects. They'd alert her to danger on the water. They'd protect their queen by numbers alone. For the first time since Mathair Mhór's hut, she felt safe. She felt like she belonged.

She wondered if Balor knew she could shift into a swan. She didn't think so. If he knew the truth, he would have trapped every last swan in all the realms to ensure she didn't get away. So what was it that he wanted from her? Was there another part of her yet to discover?

She swam through the water, her legs finally stretching and moving in a manner they'd always longed to. But even in this magnificent form, which made her feel so incredibly alive, she wanted to get back into the castle. The ability to shift into a swan didn't dissuade her from needing to kill Balor. She would find a way to get to him at his most vulnerable. She'd enter through the tunnels. The exit she had used to escape this time was likely the same one she'd used as a child. Of course, she'd have to steer clear of the branch that led to the royal washroom. The crocodiles were surely enchanted, but the wound on her leg was real enough. She didn't recall turning into a swan that night so many years ago, but then, for most of her life she had blocked the entire evening from her memory. Gallean had pushed her to remember bits and pieces of it, but she still hadn't remembered the shift.

She soon grew weary of her flock. Each time she tried to glide in the direction of the castle, they steered her away as if they knew their queen was risking exposure and they'd sworn to protect her. If she was going to get any insight on the castle, she'd have to shift back into her human form, and she wasn't quite sure how to go about doing it. Could she shift back as easily as she had transformed into the swan? It would prove a useful ability, especially while in Balor's realm. Whenever his sorcerer closed in on her location, she'd shift into a swan and swim or fly away. She'd try tomorrow in the thickets.

The moon waxed high in the night sky. Soon it would phase into the Shadow Moon. That was when the brother and sister were supposed to have arrived. Gallean had believed there were universal rules that everyone must follow in whatever realm they may be in, but the brother and sister had broken the rules. Perhaps Caer could break the rules too.

And what of the brother and sister? Gallean had said they were to join as three powers, the trí cumhacht, and that their powers would surpass his own, but was it because of her swan form or because of other powers she had yet to discover?

Her body tingled beneath the feathers when she thought of the brother. He triggered something in her that went far beyond physical attraction. Sure, he was handsome. Godlike even. But there was something beneath his exterior that spoke to her. Called to her.

She tucked her head beneath her wing and drifted off to sleep.

She tiptoed over to the sleeping figure. Her toes peeked out of from beneath her leather leggings. They reminded her of half-moons, and she knew she was human again. Her heart raced as she approached the bed. After spending a lifetime hiding in the shadows, Caer was surprised at her own boldness, but confidence surged within her. If pressed, she could shift into a swan and fly out the open window into the night. Swans may not be as swift as sparrows or as predatory as hawks, but they are strong and powerful. They are the birds of legend.

The blankets rose and fell with his breathing. She leaned in to watch his eyes dance beneath the lids. She imagined them sparkling with delight at the discovery of her there. She longed to peer at them, but waking him was a risk. Gallean had warned her not to return. He'd claimed it wasn't time for the three of them to unite.

Scott's mouth pulsed as if he was talking in his sleep or maybe kissing someone. She couldn't read minds, but the thought of him kissing another surged red hot in her veins. She dropped an image of herself into his head. His lips rose in a smile, and he let out a soft sigh.

She imagined waking him and asking him to go for a walk. He nodded and reached for her hand. In a reckless move, she let him take it. Jolts of energy shot through them. She'd gone too far. She could sense him fighting to arise from his slumber. She cloaked herself as she pulled her hand from his and ran toward the open window.

"What's your name?" he whispered into the darkness, his voice reverberating in her mind, in her soul.

"Caer," she replied as she leapt onto the windowsill.

"Caer," he sighed, rolling over in his bed as she stretched her wings and disappeared into the night.

She woke with a jerk. Her head flew out from under her wing. Foggy brained, she glanced around. She was still tucked into the middle of the flock on the embankment of the lake, exactly where she had fallen asleep.

How could that be? She'd visited the brother in the Land of Shadows. Hadn't she? Sometimes it was hard to tell the difference between what was real and what was imagined.

The rest of the flock began to stir, sensing their queen was awake. Their movement obscured her view of the castle, but it was there, nonetheless.

A burning desire to see Scott again replaced any betrayal

she felt toward him and his sister. She tilted her head toward the night sky.

In time everything would work out. It was funny how comfortable she felt in her new form. Her whole life she had been scared. Now, in this more fragile form, she felt strong. Confident. Proud.

Someday she'd return to the Land of Shadows. She'd return and kiss the brother. Many times.

As the sun rose, Caer stared at the castle. She needed to get back inside and figure out the best way to kill Balor. The washroom was clearly out—between the crocodiles and its location behind the throne room, there was no way she'd be able to kill him and disappear without alerting his guards. The bedroom then. If she mastered her shapeshifting, she could fly to his window at night, stab him in his patched eye, and disappear into the darkness.

With his death, chaos would ensue. His second in command would take over. She'd kill him too. She'd kill everyone who attempted to take control of the castle. They'd soon fear the night phantom killer. They'd never suspect a woman, much less the daughter of the former king. The tunnels would be searched in hopes of finding a shred of evidence of the killer's identity. They'd find nothing.

Every guard would fall under suspicion. Trust would disappear. Caer would strike again and again until there was no one left to kill or they abandoned the castle. Then, and only then, Caer would take her place as Queen.

Yes, it was a splendid plan—one filled with blood and revenge—but there was a crucial component that would need to be worked out before she could take another life. Her ability to shift.

She swam over to the thicket. Surprisingly, the flock

remained a distance away as if they sensed what she was about to attempt and wished to provide her with privacy. Their distance also told her she wasn't in danger. She waded between the reeds and tall grasses until her feet reached the mucky bottom. She waddled onto a raised dry bed, and glanced down at her silver necklace. It had changed from sword to chain when she swam through the channel in the tunnel. She was counting on it shifting back into the sword when she took on her human form again. If not, her plans to kill Balor while he slept would be difficult—though not impossible.

She quieted her breathing. The song of crickets and other insects filled her with confidence—it meant she was alone. In her dream, she had become human when she'd landed on Scott's window. The shift had occurred as naturally as flying when in swan form.

The memory of Scott's sleeping form filled her with longing. Overcome with desire, she reached out to touch him. Her wing of feathers transformed into an arm with skin. Her beak pulled in on itself. Her legs stretched and elongated. The tall grass on either side of her disappeared, leaving nothing but blue skies and the lake in front of her. She cracked her neck from side to side, her shift from prey to predator complete.

But it wouldn't do. She refused to rely on her attraction to a man to necessitate the shift. It was Caer who had survived on her own all those years between Mathair Mhór's death and her time with Gallean. It was Caer who had snuck into the castle and fought off the crocodiles. It was Caer who had killed a man. She swung her sword high in the air. No man would define her.

She curved the blade toward the ground in front of her as she focused on shifting back into a swan. Before the sword hit, it wrapped around her neck, her face pinched and pulled, and her arms quickly changed back into wings. The grass reappeared at her sides. She had returned to prey, but she did not feel vulnerable. She trusted her swan form to carry her far from danger. She would not be afraid. Not anymore.

With intention, she imagined herself as a human. The way the wind kissed her cheeks before a storm. The heat of a fire warming the icy veins surrounding her heart after Gallean had turned her away. The rush of adrenaline as sword met bone. Her body quickly changed back into a human. A wave of dizziness overcame her, and she fell to the ground. The sudden shift taxed her energy reserves. She would not be able to transform back and forth continually without depleting herself. She closed her eyes and rested. In human form, she was vulnerable. She pooled the last of her energy one final time to return to swan form.

Her flock soon surrounded her, sensing that their queen needed them. It allowed her to recover under their watchful eyes. She couldn't smile with a beak, but her heart and soul sang in belonging.

That night, she swam to the center of the lake. She was not alone, but she no longer minded their company. She found strength not only in her swan form but also in her flock. She stretched her neck, exposing her throat to the moonlight. The Shadow Moon was to signal the brother and sister's arrival. Their early appearance had altered her path. She had denied her true nature for many years. Gallean had tried to force her into remembering but she'd refused. It was her anger that led her to open the portal and return to her homeland. It was her need for revenge that led her to the castle. But it was her own self that led her to her swan.

The moon drifted into darkness as the Earth's umbra cast a shadow upon it. The Shadow Moon brought her clarity.

Her ability to visit the brother in his dreams, her visions of the future she never understood so she ignored them instead, even her ability to make a portal in a land where magic could not occur—these gifts marked her not only as a shapeshifting swan, they marked her as a goddess. Her father was not just a mortal king, he was a god, and even he could not withstand Balor on his own.

She realized what she needed to do. She also needed help, and she knew who to ask.

20

SIX OF PENTACLES

*S*cott ignored the guilt coursing through him as he climbed down the stairs to breakfast. Gallean had probably figured out that he was the one who had talked Gigi into trying to escape. He didn't know if Gallean could read minds like Gigi, or if he was a master in studying body language like Granda, but he knew the wizard would piece together the truth.

In a way he was surprised Gigi hadn't suggested leaving earlier in the week, given her love of rebellion. But then, she was distracted. The dark circles under her eyes told a story. He knew the tale included Alaric, and maybe Lizzie too, but he didn't think it would end with, "and they lived happily ever after." He wished it would for Gigi, but if her recent past was any indication, she'd find a way to screw it up. It didn't matter that she was a reincarnated goddess. In this life, her mistakes defined her.

Scott didn't remember any of his past incarnations. He suspected that he didn't leave the Otherworld often because his true love lived there with him. She came to him again last night after they had returned to the keep and settled in for the night. When she touched him, love coursed through them so intensely it almost felt real. He knew the dreams weren't real though, that she hadn't really come to him, but he wished she had. Maybe then he'd remember more of his past lives. Maybe he'd figure out who he was supposed to be in this one.

He didn't understand the anger that often replaced his reason. In Vernal Falls he rarely got upset. He prided himself on his patience and his ability to keep Gi under control, but here in the Shadow Realm, anger flashed through him. He got so frustrated with his inability to control his magic. He knew Gallean's tai chi-judo-yoga moves helped to encapsulate magic and pull and manipulate it into a form meeting the individual's needs but, come on. How long did it take to master the movement?

Gallean would tell him it took years, and that patience was necessary, but they didn't have years. Alaric had been missing for a while now, and Lizzie was somehow alive but in werewolf form. Gigi had lasted much longer in her energy training than he thought she could, but then, she always surprised him. She'd explode, rip a locker to shreds, try to hurt herself too, then manage to pull herself together and seem perfectly "normal" faster than anyone he knew. Ever since she had embraced her goddess-ness on the night of Samhain, there was a certain knowing about her. She had tried to play the "I-was-lying-to-Clayone" card and pretend she wasn't the goddess. He didn't know why she had lied about it, but then she often lied for the pure joy of it. He liked to believe that she didn't lie to him, but he suspected she did. Now that she had acknowledged the goddess side of her, there was a confident aura surrounding her.

Truth to be told, Gi made Scott feel better just by being in the Shadow Realm with him. For all her faults, and she had many, she was his best friend. She brought out the best in him in a way no one else could. He knew she wasn't going to stay here as long as he was. It was foretold that they would be separated. He was sure Gigi assumed the worst—that she was going to die and that the world would never fully recover from her departure. But that wasn't it. She'd find some loophole so she could go after Alaric, and he'd be stuck here with Gallean and only his dreams of Caer because he couldn't go in search of her. The wizard had said she'd come when she was ready. Scott wished she'd hurry.

Gallean was waiting for him in the courtyard. The wizard reminded him of one of the wild men from dad's Celtic folktales. His ability to shapeshift and his gift of magic made him extremely powerful. Had it really been mastering those energy movements here that had made him the most powerful wizard in the universe? But if he couldn't practice magic here, did anyone really know just how powerful he was?

"I appreciate you joining me this morning. I thought perhaps you'd stay in your room and sulk like your sister," he said.

Scott didn't detect any reprimand regarding Gigi's behavior, merely the mention that she wasn't with them—which was good because Gi would unleash major attitude if the wizard attempted to discipline her. Of all the adults they'd met since they arrived in Ireland, Gallean seemed the least impressed that they were reincarnated gods. Maybe impressed was the wrong word. Gallean didn't permit teenage misbehavior and attitude regardless of their god stature. Clarissa and Granda liked to suggest an appropriate action or reaction, but they rarely made them do something they didn't want to do, like work on energy dancing for hours on end.

"She came to you again last night, didn't she?"

Scott's stomach lurched. At this rate he'd have to be

careful what he ate for breakfast. He nodded as his answer. The less he talked about her aloud, the better he'd be able to deal with it.

"In what form does she arrive?"

Scott did not feel like talking about Caer this morning. It would just make him more desperate to find her.

"As a human, but then she flies out the window as a swan."

Gallean raised his fingers to his chin. Usually when the wizard fell into this contemplative silence, Scott and Gi would sit at the table, unsure of what they should do. But this morning, without Gigi to roll his eyes with, he had only Gallean.

"What does that mean?"

Gallean removed his fingers from his chin and stared at him. "I believe she's coming to terms with her new form, and she's struggling with her ability to shift and reshift. The change can be a painful, tiresome practice, but she is determined to master it."

Scott stiffened. Granted he didn't know Caer in her human or swan form, he *knew* her. "Is there anything we can do to help her? You're a shapeshifter. Can't you instruct her how to best go about it?"

"She's not afraid of the pain of the shift, though shifts close together will weaken her for the immediate future. Her greatest concern is the danger she faces. She's afraid to alert others of her presence. But her confidence is growing. Soon, she will embrace her true nature, and she will become a powerful ally to you."

Scott jumped up. "She's in danger? Who's after her?" The protective side of him made it impossible to stand still, let alone listen to the wizard. He was a man of action, and he protected those in need.

"There is only one who seeks her. One who knows not of

171

her swan form, but he knows she is a reincarnated goddess, and he'll stop at nothing to collect her."

Scott didn't care that she was a swan or a reincarnated goddess. He wouldn't rest until he found her, and he'd protect her the best way he knew how. He'd eliminate the person threatening her.

"Who? Who is it? I'll kill him. I will absolutely kill him."

Gallean waved his hands at Scott as if fanning off his temper and his testosterone—of which he would do neither.

"A man will not kill him. It is foretold it will be a woman."

He was so tired of prophecies and predictions. Couldn't people just do or not do something? Why did there have to be an "It is foretold . . ."? That line made him want to break something. It also made him sick because he knew who the subject of that particular prophecy was.

"Caer."

"Indeed."

"What is the bastard's name?"

"Balor."

It took Scott several long minutes to recover. He only snapped out of his shocked state because Gi knocked into him when she finally came downstairs.

"What the feck is wrong with you?" she said, shoving him again for good measure.

"Balor is after Caer," he whispered.

Again Balor had erupted into their lives, pulling the three into a battle against him, because Scott would fight him to protect Caer. He didn't care about prophecies and who was designated to kill or not kill—he'd kill the monster before Caer even got the chance.

If Breas had been successful in bringing Balor over when the veil was thin on the night of Samhain, it would mean that

Caer was safe for the time being. She was in the Shadow Realm, or whatever realm her lake was in—far away from the Earthly Realm. Scott would continue his training with Gallean, and when he was ready, he'd take a portal with Gigi and kill the bastard who was after his love.

"That's where things get complicated," Gallean said.

Gigi jumped up and seated herself on the table, putting herself above them. Not because she wanted to prove that she was better than them, but because she still needed to express her rebel nature in subversive ways, such as sitting on an all-powerful wizard's table.

"Complicated? What the feck is complicated? We kill Balor and save the world and Scott's swan."

Two could play at Gi's game. "What about your wolf?"

She popped a handful of berries into her mouth. "I don't think he plays a part in this."

"There are many things you both have yet to understand."

Scott stared at the wizard. "Then teach us. Help us understand."

Gallean stood up and waved for them to follow. "It is better if I show you."

He led them into a library of sorts. Wall to wall, floor to ceiling shelves, loaded with ancient volumes and glass specimen jars containing collections from nature—crystals, fungi, dried berries, and on and on. There were also more weird contraptions than he'd ever seen before. The library reminded him of his and Gigi's rooms at the keep, but instead of beds, there were tables stacked with books and papers and everything one could imagine in a wizard's library, along with thousands of things one couldn't imagine.

The wizard began flipping through a large stack of maps. "I do not believe either of you have seen a map of our worlds before."

Scott didn't like how that sounded. A map of *our* worlds,

as if the wizard's Shadow Realm was somehow aligned with the world they'd left behind, which was somehow aligned with wherever Caer was.

Gi snapped her fingers. It was a habit she'd adopted recently so she wouldn't accidentally create a fireball, although it didn't matter in the Shadow Realm. "We've seen a map of Ireland before. We tried to find Alaric with it. To no success, I might add."

Gallean pulled apart several maps as if opening a book. "The reason is because you used a modern map of Ireland to try to locate beings that are magically enhanced."

Scott added a heavy log to the corner to settle the pages. "And you're suggesting that was not the best way to go about doing it?"

"I'm not just suggesting it; I assure you it was the wrong way."

Gigi stiffened. His sister never did like being told she'd done something wrong. Of course, she intentionally broke rules all the time, but in this case she thought she had used all the means within her power to find Alaric. Gallean's claim was a major blow to not only her ego, but her heart.

"If you've got a better way, give it up," she said.

Gallean stood above the map. He pulled in his hands, pushed them below his hips, raised them, then pushed them out at the map to press down the remaining edges. It was hard to believe that he wasn't conducting magic. His manipulation of energy simulated what Scott had come to understand was earthly magic. Maybe his assumptions on that subject were wrong as well.

"You'll notice the outline of the country you recognize as Ireland."

They followed his finger as he skimmed over the boundary before settling on an island in the upper right corner.

"You may also be familiar with the Isle of Man?"

Gigi pulled her hands to her chest and widened her eyes as if her words weren't going to tell him exactly what she was thinking. "Wow. I mean, you are a wise wizard. You're right. We've been going about our search all wrong."

His sister was masterfully skilled at sarcasm. It really was a gift. But this time, she'd overlooked the obvious.

"Gi, look," Scott said, pointing to another island south of the Isle of Man and closer to Ireland. "That wasn't on our map."

She bent next to him as they studied it. The map used the ancient mapmaking notations of a triangle without a base for mountains, thick circles with bases for trees, and other rudimentary drawings that left the viewer with little doubt what each symbol stood for. She stabbed it with her finger. "What is this place? Where is it?"

Gallean removed her finger with a sweep of his hand without even touching it. "I'd ask for care when examining my maps."

Gigi rolled her eyes. "Apologies. Now where is it? Can we get there by boat?"

"Patience. This island you already know, because you are on it."

Scott pried himself away from the map to study Gallean. "The Shadow Realm is on maps?"

Gallean held up a finger. "On this map, and perhaps one or two others. But if you look closely, you'll find it's not called the Shadow Realm. That title sounds Otherworldly, and I assure you, we are very much in your world."

Gi's patience was stretched to its limitations. They were fortunate that she could not fully erupt in Gallean's keep. "Then what is the name of it?"

Scott lightly traced the title with his finger. "The Land of Shadows."

"Correct," the wizard nodded at him.

"Why is it not on the maps? How did Granda and Clarissa know of it?"

"Clarissa knew of it long ago when she was—well, I guess she was about your age. Brigit sent her here so I could train her."

Gi raised an eyebrow. "You trained Clarissa?"

"I did, along with many others for centuries. More recently, I haven't been taking on new students, but you two interested me."

"You wanted to train reincarnated gods—I get it. You wanted to add 'How to Train Freaks' to your training manuals," Gi growled.

His sister was gearing up for a fight. Every time her uniqueness was mentioned, she took it as a slight against her fundamental character.

"He means nothing of the sort, sis." He turned to stare at the wizard. "You sense something big coming. Are you scared?"

The wizard shifted uncomfortably. "I'm not alarmed. I'm merely concerned."

"Why isn't the Land of Shadows on the maps?"

Gallean laid another map on top of it. It was a more recent edition than the original. He pointed at where the Land of Shadows was on the other one. "It's beginning to be."

Scott bent over again to study it. Beneath heavy clouds and waves, the faint outline of the Land of Shadows was beginning to appear. "What does it mean?"

Gigi uncrossed her arms and bent over to look.

The muscles beneath Gallean's jaw feathered. "It means the magical mist that keeps this island hidden from the rest of the world is lifting."

"Why?" His sister glanced up at the wizard in alarm. As

much as she pretended not to care about anything, she cared about everything.

Gallean flopped down in his chair and sighed. "That storm your grandfather and Clarissa have warned you about?"

"Yes," they said together.

"It's coming here too."

He really wasn't giving them much to work with.

"And what's the cause of it?"

Gallean pulled back the two maps to reveal another map, a bottom layer of the ancient one. "Look again."

Scott peered over at it with Gigi. The Isle of Man was there, along with the Land of Shadows. The mainland was also intact with the mountains, grassy knolls, forests, and what appeared to be magical boundaries—like around Newgrange. That must be why they couldn't cross the barrier there. He'd ask Gallean about that later, but there was a more pressing issue. On this map the lakes—well, loughs—were filled with terrible monsters and sea creatures spilling out of them. "What does this mean?"

"It means the Fomorians have found a way out, and they are planning to take back Ireland for their own."

Boots scraped across the windowsill. All three turned. Scott had discovered many surprising things so far this morning, but this was the biggest surprise of all.

21

ACE OF CUPS

*C*aer hopped down from the open window. "It also means the old wizard has known the battle was approaching for all this time, and yet he's done nothing but teach you to move balls of energy around."

The sister turned to her and smiled. "Finally, someone who speaks my language."

Caer approached the table. After killing the man in the alley, her incident with the crocodiles, and then her shapeshifting, along with still being pissed off at Gallean for choosing the siblings over her, she was in no mood for niceties. She whipped her sword from behind her back and held it to the sister's throat. "Do not mistake my cordial greeting as a sign of friendship."

The sister swallowed. Good. She should quake in Caer's presence.

"Actually, you've just sealed her friendship. If you had passed her a note or thrown her a warm greeting, she'd hate you for it. Violent acts elicit her respect."

Caer yanked her sword from the sister's neck and swung it to the brother's. "And what does this greeting say to you?"

He swallowed. Good. She wanted to unnerve him for all he'd put her through.

"I meant no harm when I suggested you and Gigi were now friends. I just wanted you to be aware that she's a twisted soul."

"Hey," the sister said. "That hurt. And I am not twisted."

His green eyes sparkled at Caer, speaking of mischief and longing. He was entirely too comfortable with a sword to his throat. She poked a little harder.

"Perhaps I should introduce myself. I'm Scott."

He offered her his hand. She stared at it. She'd longed to feel his touch for many weeks, and now, in person, she wanted nothing more than to slice his head off. He made her feel weak.

"Love does not weaken," Gallean said, as he gently gripped the handle and pulled the sword from Scott's neck. "It only strengthens."

"What do you know of love?" she growled, reaching for one of the throwing knives on her belt. She rarely used them, preferring the one in her boot, but she'd make an exception for the wizard.

The sister gasped. Caer suspected she was a mind reader. Good. It would make them get along much better—the sister would know what she wanted and would follow her command.

The wizard, however, laughed at her. His disregard infuriated her even more. "You think you're going to skewer me with your toys?"

She pulled one of her knives out. The sunlight glinted off the blade. "They're not toys," she said through gritted teeth.

"In my keep they are toys. Search within yourself. You do not have the will to kill me."

"I had the will to kill the man in the alley. Did you see

that, or were you too distracted with your new students to keep an eye on me?"

His eyes softened. "You were provoked. You did what you needed to do in order to protect yourself."

"I am provoked right now, so would that mean killing you was necessary to protect myself?"

The brother approached her. He didn't hesitate and he didn't waver.

"Scott!" the sister warned.

He stopped in front of her, putting himself at great risk.

"Caer," he whispered, drawing up his hands and tracing the lines of her face. "I cannot believe it's really you."

She swallowed. She didn't expect him to leave his midsection unguarded. She could run her knife straight through him, shift into a swan, and fly out the window.

"Don't fly away from me this time," he said in a husky undertone that only she could hear. His voice did something to her own midsection. It was the same tingly sensation she had wanted the man at the pub to quench. Before her stood the cause of it. Her mind fluttered through a variety of next steps, but really, there was only one thing she wanted to do.

The knife clattered to the stone floor as she wrapped her hands around his neck and pulled his lips to hers.

Thunder rumbled outside as a shot of lightning hit the floor beside them.

"Well, you don't see that every day," the sister said. "And I'd appreciate you calling me Gigi rather than labeling me 'the sister' in your head. It's really emotionally removed."

Scott backed away from Caer's lips, but his hand wrapped around hers. "Says the epitome of emotionally removed."

Gigi's lips twitched. "Well, I suppose perhaps I am again. What with my boyfriend being brainwashed by my best friend."

Scott leaned into Caer's ear. "Don't mind her."

His voice tickled her neck. Her head wanted to fold into him, but it would not do to reveal the way her body reacted to him.

"Too late," Gigi said. "He is well aware of his effect on you."

She stiffened as she looked at Gigi. "It's rude to invade other people's minds."

Gigi waved at her. "I try not to, but sometimes a person's thoughts scream at me. I can't help but interrupt. Now, before our happy trio joined together, Gallean was about to reveal something to us."

The old wizard stood watching the three of them with his mouth wide open.

"Gallean?" Gigi said again. "We're waiting . . ."

He blinked, bringing himself to the present. He was clearly unnerved. "First, Caer, how is it you were able to arrive here?"

Scott squeezed her hand. It warmed her cheeks. He was familiar to her, but that didn't take the shyness away. She had interacted so little with people, aside from Mathair Mhór and Gallean, that she hardly knew how to act or what to say.

Gigi elbowed her. "Don't worry. I'll show you."

"I still have my sword, you know."

Gigi touched the red mark on her neck. "Oh, I am well aware of your sword skills. Maybe you shouldn't think so loudly."

"Gi, be nice to her," Scott warned.

"I am being nice. Maybe if you gave her some room, she wouldn't be so uncomfortable."

Scott turned to her. "Am I making you uncomfortable?"

She didn't want to lie to him, but the truth was, if she had any chance of remembering what Gallean was about to tell them, she needed to be able to get air into her brain. "A little," she admitted.

He withdrew his hand from hers. "As long as you don't leave, take all the time you need."

Caer pursed her lips as she glared at the wizard. Anger did help her think more clearly. "The same way Gigi and Scott arrived early."

He pulled his fingers to his chin. "You made a portal."

"You knew I could. I've done it before, haven't I? It's how I got here after Balor burned down Mathair Mhór's hut. It's how I was able to go back to my father's castle after you kicked me out. I didn't understand it when I first arrived on the banks of the lake, but I eventually realized my abilities. Good thing too, because I made a startling discovery."

A heavy wind swept into the room and swirled around Gallean. "And what is that?"

She slammed her fist into the map table. She really wanted to slam it into his face, but she didn't want to anger the wizard more than he appeared to be. The wizard she could take. The bear? Well, she wasn't half as confident.

"You knew Balor wasn't at my father's castle. That's why you sent me away. You knew I'd go there. You wanted to distract me while they were here so you could train them without worrying about me."

Gallean said nothing. He did nothing.

She stomped over to him. He was still seated, but they stood eye to eye. "I almost got killed in the royal washroom."

"What?" Scott said approaching her.

She threw up her hand to stop him. He backed away.

Gallean stared at her. "But you didn't."

"Did you know about the crocodiles that attacked me? I only got away because . . ."

"Because you embraced your shapeshifting nature."

"I didn't embrace it so much as—"

"If you hadn't shifted into the swan, you would have become crocodile soup?" Gigi offered.

"Something like that. Why, Gallean? Why do you subject me to these 'lessons'? You show them how to move energy around, but you plunge me into life-threatening situations in which I need to fight in order to survive."

Gallean pushed himself up from the chair. She backpedaled away from him as he approached his full height and towered over her. "You've lived in denial long enough. I tried to force it out of you, but you resisted. You needed to either embrace your shapeshifting nature or perish."

"At Lake of the Dragon Mouth, under the Shadow Moon, understanding came to me. I am not just a swan shapeshifter. I am a goddess. That's why I can create portals."

"That ability is one small aspect of it."

Can you make one now? Gigi dropped the question in her head.

"You cannot make a portal here," Gallean warned her. "Do not even try."

Please. I need to get home. I need to find Alaric.

Caer felt Gigi's need. She knew it well, and she would not make her suffer any longer if she could help it.

If the wizard sensed what she was about to do, he'd stop her immediately. Caer yanked out her sword, arced it through the air, and sliced open a portal. Gigi didn't move as quickly as she'd have liked. She shoved her through and jerked the sword out to shut it.

"What have you done?" Gallean whispered.

"What I would have done from the beginning if I had known the truth of my true natures," she hissed through clenched teeth.

"Gigi," Scott cried, dropping to his knees in front of the space where his sister had disappeared.

She remembered how it felt to lose someone she loved, but unlike her story endings, he'd be rejoined with his sister someday, and together they'd form the trí cumhacht.

"It's time for you to train us, wizard."

Something feral replaced the sadness in Scott's eyes as he stood up and lunged in her direction. He stopped just inches from her. "How could you send her away? She's all alone. The werewolves will kill her."

Caer stumbled back from him. "Werewolves?"

"Balor isn't the only monster out there," he growled, storming past her.

"No, he isn't," Gallean said beside her, "and without Gigi and her abilities, I don't know if you and Scott can take Balor before he frees his armies."

Her anger returned with a vengeance. "My father's death will be avenged. I'll make sure of it."

That night, she lay in Gigi's bed, but she couldn't sleep. The mattress was entirely too soft and the room too warm. She longed for her cave or for a restful night on the lake with her flock, but she didn't want to leave Gallean's keep. Truth be told, she didn't want to put more distance between her and Scott than the giant ravine she had already created after she'd ripped open the portal and shoved Gigi into it. She knew that, from his point of view, it looked like she wanted to get rid of his sister. But Gigi had begged her, and something about her pleading voice triggered sympathy in Caer. She too had been alone, wanting someone to help her so many times she had lost count. She had tried to explain it to Scott that afternoon, but he had ignored her knocks and refused to return to the courtyard even when Gallean called him for a training session.

She had thought about shifting into a swan and flying into his room, but it was wrong to invade his privacy, especially in the daytime when he was awake. And now that they had met, visiting his room at night felt far too intimate for her liking, especially after their kiss.

She traced her fingers along her lips, remembering the way it felt when she'd kissed him. She had dreamt of him many nights since she first saw him in the seomra de rúin. They'd shared a history together when they were first upon the earthly plane and had continued their love into the Otherworld. Her restful sleep with her flock had triggered many memories for her.

She crawled out of the bed and made a nest on the floor. She began drifting off to sleep when she heard a creak outside her door. Her hearing along with the rest of her senses was attuned to discover even the slightest of movements. She hadn't survived in the wild for years on her own without the ability to protect herself. Her ears perked as she listened for who might be outside her door. She doubted it was Gallean. Although he'd begun their knife-throwing session annoyed at Caer for sending Gigi away, by the end he seemed to enjoy the rigorous nature of their training. He probably hadn't used certain muscles since Scott and Gigi had arrived. His body savored the movement of them.

Could it be Scott? Her heart raced as she remembered their kiss from the afternoon. She was glad she had initiated it, but she didn't know if she was brave enough to try it again. Especially now that he was upset with her for sending his sister away.

The floor creaked again. It must be him. She sucked in a breath and tiptoed over to the door. Resting her ear against the wood, she listened for a heartbeat or his breath or maybe a whisper calling for her like he'd done when she'd come to the keep and visited him in his sleep. He thought it had been a dream. She still wasn't sure, but together, the moment was real.

She rested her hand on the door handle. Should she open

it and come face to face with him or wait for him to come to her? She could hear his quiet breaths outside the door and imagined them each resting a hand on the very same spot, their cheeks touching as they listened to each other's heartbeat.

Eventually she must have fallen asleep. When she woke, she found herself curled up in a ball, her hand and cheek still pressing against the door. She wasn't sure what would come of their training sessions today, but she hoped that the anger and resentment he felt for her had disappeared with the morning dew.

She ducked her head as she approached the table where Gallean and Scott sat talking as they broke their fast together.

"Good morning, Caer," Gallean said, "I presume you slept well."

Her cheeks flushed hotly. She suspected the wizard knew where she had slept. She nodded, afraid her voice would betray her.

"And you, Scott? Did you sleep well?"

She peeked at him out of the corner of her eye. He swallowed hard, then cleared his throat as he fidgeted with the berries on his plate. He finally glanced over at her before answering the wizard.

"I did."

A small smile crept across her face. She tried to hide it as she reached for some dried meat, but if either one of them were looking at her, they'd know the cause of it.

"Splendid. Today I thought we'd continue where Caer and I left off yesterday. Caer, your aim is good, but one always needs practice. I'd like you to work on throwing a spear as well."

She nodded, pleased that the wizard had decided to continue with her weaponry training rather than making her master his rhythmic dance.

"Scott, you will work on throwing knives into a target, and depending on your skill, we will progress from there."

Scott pushed away from the table. "I had assumed we'd open a portal and fetch Gigi."

Gallean stood up and wiped the crumbs off his shirt. "You assumed incorrectly. With the skills your sister acquired during her stay, she is more than ready to continue on her journey."

Caer watched as the air swirled around Scott. It was as if his emotions were causing an energy shift, but it wasn't like when she pulled the energy to become invisible.

"You call learning how to move energy balls a preparation for battle?" he asked.

Gallean stalked over to him. Though the wizard towered over Scott, Scott didn't appear concerned, and the swirling air continued to build.

"As you know, your sister is not capable of causing harm to humans with her magic or a weapon. She will play a part in the upcoming battle, but it won't be with a sword, knife, or spear. If she had remained in the Land of Shadows much longer, she would have faded. Humanity gives her life. She needs to touch and savor them."

"What about the werewolves that want to kill her?"

"They are part human too. Your sister is powerful. She has other means to protect herself that I can no longer teach her. She will either discover them by instinct and necessity or perish trying."

Scott collapsed to his knees. "Perish? As in die?"

Gallean rested his hands on Scott's shoulders. "Brigit takes that risk each time she reincarnates. She knows the potential ramifications, but she chooses to do it anyway. If she survives, she will be more powerful than all the gods once again."

"But what about the Fomorians?"

"They are of an ancient line of gods. Her magic, if she chooses to use it, will work against them."

"So that leaves us to fight?" he said, gesturing to himself and Caer.

Gallean removed his hands from Scott's shoulders and lifted his chin instead. "Do not be afraid to say her name. It is not her fault Gigi left. Gigi chose to. Caer merely supplied her with the path to do so. You should thank her."

Scott's eyes slid over to hers. A rush of warmth consumed her body.

"Caer, thank you."

Her midsection tingled again. She needed to learn to control her physical reactions to him. She didn't want him holding extra powers over her, but she did appreciate his gratitude.

"Scott, you are welcome."

The wizard raised his hands, and knives appeared in them. "Let's begin."

Caer's fingers worked the knives and guided them into the target. Each time, she imagined Balor's eye opening, and each time, her blades found their mark. It would take discipline and determination to gain access to Balor. Her plan of flying in and out of the castle, killing as she went, was ill conceived. She was a warrior. A warrior of strong mind and body. One capable of a well-formed battle strategy. Her short visit to her father's castle had proved that she was not adequately prepared to find him even at his most vulnerable, at least not alone. But with Scott as her training partner and Gallean as her teacher, she just might find her target.

She launched a ten-foot spear across the courtyard. It

soared through the air three hundred paces before sticking into the bullseye.

"Well done, Caer. Well done," Gallean said, clapping her on the back.

Scott stared at her. She tingled again, but this time from the adrenaline that coursed through her as the spear had found its mark. It gave her confidence that she would succeed in her mission.

If she wanted to survive, she'd have to.

THE END

~

Reviews are like dance parties. Sometimes awkward, sometimes spastic, but someone's got to get them started!

Keep reading for an excerpt of
Oak Moon: The Goddess Chronicles Book Five

JOIN THE KOVEN

Read Clarissa and Carman's origin story, The Druids Sisters of the Gallicennial, FREE by signing up for K's Koven. Be the FIRST to find out about new releases from Best-Selling Author, K.B. Anne. PLUS, receive Newsletter Subscriber Only Bonus Content, insight on Celtic Mythology, Druids, Witches, Werewolves, and Magic, and so much more! Join K's Koven today!

SHADOW MOON TAROT CARD INDEX

Caer's Chapters are Tarot Cards. @Enchanted.Endeavors on Instagram pulled a card each day I wrote (or so it seemed.) The card always matched up with the scene with alarming accuracy. I considered adding them as a quote at the start of Caer's Chapters, but I didn't want to detract from her story. I also didn't want to change Jayse's words. Enjoy!

Ace of Cups - A new family connection or blossoming romance. It is exciting – fluttery even – and you are so glad to have met someone with whom you can share a special connection. Give yourself permission to open yourself to giving and receiving unconditional love, and you will notice that affection flows effortlessly when you are in this loving state of mind.

Nine of Wands – This card appears when you feel battered and bruised, having gone through huge struggles along your path. Just when you think you are making progress, you suffer another setback. This card asks you to trust that this is merely a test of your resilience, and know that every time you overcome an obstacle, you are getting stronger.

The Nine of Wands encourages you to keep pushing – you are so close to the finish line. Even if you want to give up, this is your final challenge before you reach your goal, so don't let go of your hopes and dreams when you are so close to making them a reality.

Queen of Swords – This card combines the intellectual power of the suit of Swords with the maturity and receptiveness of the Queen.

You may be approached by someone in your day who is seeking clarity. When interacting with others, you will not tolerate mistruths or excessive 'fluff'. You prefer to get to the heart of the matter without engaging in chit-chat or gossip.

You are a quick thinker and highly perceptive, piercing through the noise and confusion to get straight to the point. You are upfront and honest in your views, and you expect the same from others.

Seven of Swords - Take care, you may be the victim of someone else's betrayal. Others are not being candid with you, and you may be unaware of their lies and deception. You may trust someone who then turns out to be running their own agenda, leaving you high and dry. Look out for any sneaky behaviour and listen to your intuition when something does not feel right or seems too good to be true.

This card also indicates that you are trying to escape from a situation you've gotten yourself into, instead of dealing with it head on, you are running from it, or pushing it to the bottom of the pile. This card suggests you need to take the time do deal with the mess before moving on.

Six of Pentacles - this card suggests that you offer up your time, energy, love and support to those who are in need. Giving your time or your wisdom is often just as fulfilling as giving away money or gifts and the gift of your presence is received just as well, if not better. .

You may wonder if you can truly afford to give to others, the advice of the Six of Pentacles is to trust that everything you do is appreciated and will come back to you times three.

Six of Pentacles REVERSED - A little self-care will go a long way, especially if you have been in giving mode for a long time. This card also shows that you may be giving to others freely whilst not getting the same back.

If you are struggling yourself, be careful that you do not over-commit yourself to others who seek your help. Take care of you, you are worth your own time.

Two of Cups - This card suggests an entering of a new partnership, perhaps with a lover, friend or business partner. You are both focused on creating a relationship that is mutually beneficial, one that will create a win-win situation for both parties. You see 'eye to eye' and appreciate what each other can bring to the table.

Two of Wands - You may be considering your longer-term goals and aspirations and are ready to plan for what you need to do to achieve them. You have already come so far, and now you feel ready for a change – this time with your long-term future in mind. You may be contemplating overseas travel, further education or a significant career switch to expand your horizons beyond your immediate environment. With careful planning and a moderated approach, you will set yourself up for success.

The Hanged Man - This card can sometimes reflect that you are feeling stuck or restricted in your life. What is holding you in this 'stuck' position? What is preventing you from moving forward? On one level, the Hanged Man is asking you pause and take a look at things from another perspective which may show you another path.

The Lovers - is often a sign that you are facing a moral dilemma and must consider all consequences before acting. Your values system is being challenged, and you are being called to take the higher path, even if it is difficult. Do not carry out a decision based on fear or worry or guilt or shame. Now, more than ever, you must choose love – love for yourself, love for others and love for the Universe. Choose the best version of yourself.

The Magician - The time is now! Now is the perfect time to bring that plan, idea or thought into action! You have all the tools you need to make this happen, with a bit of work and belief in yourself you can do it!

The World - A long-term project, period of study, relationship or career has come to completion, you are now reveling in the sense accomplishment. This could represent a graduation, marriage, the birth of a child or achieving a long-held dream. Everything has come together, and you are in the right place, doing the right thing, achieving what you have envisioned.

KB Anne's Challenge: Go back and read SHADOW MOON with these cards in mind.
Freaky similarity, huh?
Thank you Jayse, @enchanted.endeavors for your universal help with Caer's Chapters.

The Goddess Chronicles (COMPLETE)
Wide Awake: The Goddess Chronicles Book 1
Blood Moon: The Goddess Chronicles Book 2
Dark Moon: The Goddess Chronicles Book 3
Shadow Moon: The Goddess Chronicles Book 4
Oak Moon: The Goddess Chronicles Book 5
Storm Moon: The Goddess Chronicles Book 6
The Goddess Chronicles Books 1-3 Boxset
The Goddess Chronicles Books 4-6 Boxset

The Silver Fae Series (COMPLETE)
Throne of Silver: Silver Fae 1
Silver Fae Hunter: Silver Fae 2
Heirs of Wings and Shadows: Silver Fae 3
Court of Wings and Shadows: Silver Fae 4
Crown of Flames: Silver Fae 5

ABOUT THE AUTHOR

Evil author person causing book hangovers since 2018. Known to erupt into malevolent laughter fits while she writes urban fantasy featuring fierce females, swoon worthy heroes who actually listen, and explosive action because everyone needs excitement in their lives.

She writes the best-selling urban fantasy series, *The Goddess Chronicles* and *The Silver Fae* Series. She has a thing for drool worthy wolf shapeshifters. Who doesn't?

She lives in Northeast PA with 3 goblins, a task master, 2 hell hound overlords, and 2 unicorns—though sadly they don't fart rainbow glitter. The Goddess Chronicles and Silver Fae Series are ready for your consumption. Warning: May cause book hangovers.

Visit her website for more information or to contact her at kbanne.com.

Contact info:
www.KBAnne.com
kim@kbanne.com

facebook.com/KBAnneWrite
twitter.com/KBAnneWrite
instagram.com/KBAnneWrite

BESTSELLING AUTHOR
K.B. ANNE

OAK MOON

THE GODDESS CHRONICLES - BOOK FIVE

OAK MOON: THE GODDESS
CHRONICLES BOOK 5

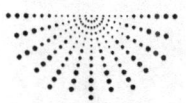

1

FIRE IS FRIEND

*F*ire is friend. Or at least it seems to be at the moment. And so far it keeps Breas and the Fomorian witch in the form of my high school nemesis, Kensey, along with the rest of the mindless swarms at bay while I figure out what we should do next. My fire shield encircles us along with the entire coven and what's left of Clarissa's cottage.

Alaric's green eyes find me. Thank the gods that the nightlock-imbued crystal necklace I threw around his neck as the Oak Moon reached its apex kept him from turning into a werewolf and tearing out my throat. As a werewolf, he isn't in control of his actions and would mourn killing me later. I'd mourn my death too, but still, stopping the change in the first place is much better. Why deal with the messy side effects? There's got to be a way to tame the wolf side of him, but today is not the day to enter him into wolf obedience school.

"As long as this fire continues to burn, we're trapped here," he shouts to me, scanning the fire shield to ensure it remains in place.

"I know, but I can't actually harm any living being, so until we figure out a Plan F.U., this is all I've got. Look on the bright side, at least I can create fire to keep our enemies out."

"Since returning from the seomra de rúin, I've had more than enough fire, thank you very much," he grumbles.

He's so cute when he's annoyed. Positively scrumptious.

Caer stands at attention on the other side of me. "There are many enemies here, but it is nothing compared to what Scott and I faced earlier."

She's not lying. The battle in the Shadow Realm reminded me of a *Clash of the Titans*–esque battle, with both Scott and Caer chopping off heads and *not* taking numbers. Medusa's fighting skills had nothing on Caer. (Although Medusa's stony expression packed a weighty punch reminiscent of Balor. The two should have a staring contest and save the rest of us a lot of trouble.)

"Any ideas what we should do next?" Scott asks on the far side of Caer.

Breas's eyes fall to the handle of Scott's sword. I got up close and personal with Scott's sword during our seomra de rúin visit to the Shadow Realm, but I hadn't noticed its ruby-encrusted handle. Where have I seen that before?

Caer grips her own sword's handle beside me, and I realize why Scott's looks familiar.

"Did you two purchase matching swords? It's kinda adorable."

She arcs her blade through the air. "There is nothing adorable about a weapon that can slice an enemy's head off."

Scott inches away from her, obviously familiar with her tendency to swing her sword around and probably not wanting to test their tenuous-at-best relationship—his words not mine.

"The swords were wedding presents given to our godly

forms," he says. "They return to us in every reincarnation and in time of need."

A werewolf lunges at the fire shield. As his body hits it, he yelps in pain and gets launched backward, his body aflame.

"We're in need of all the help we can get," Alaric says through clenched teeth, staring at the collapsed wolf.

Apparently, I can inadvertently hurt a living being if he or she were to propel themselves at one of my fire shields, although I don't feel as satisfied that I hurt someone as I thought I would be.

I step over to Alaric. "Can you retake command of your pack? Tell them to fight with us instead of against us? It would increase our odds."

More wolf eyes flash on the other side of the flames. "The whole pack's here," he whispers.

"And they've brought friends," Scott says. "Or your pack is much bigger than I thought it was."

Alaric crouches into a more combative lunge. "No. Declan's been recruiting."

My thoughts return to all the cells under the cavern. "Or Carman's made more."

He stiffens. "She knows how to make them?"

My gaze slides over to Maddie. He ever-so-slightly raises his shoulders in an I-guess-he-doesn't-know kind of way. From what Maddie told me, Alaric bit and created most of their pack, but apparently he was spelled by Carman to do it and possesses no memory of it—which fit his claims when he first showed up in my room at Granda's in the middle of the night all those weeks ago and acted like he didn't know how he got there. His attraction to me probably made it easier for Carman to spell him.

But Alaric was imprisoned in Brigit's shrine with his father for weeks. He couldn't have been spelled to create new ones.

However, there was another child of Clayone available, and "recruits" could have been sent into the shrine via the tunnel.

"Alaric, did anyone come to visit your dad while you were in the shrine?"

He blinks in surprise at my question. "Not that I remember. And I don't remember smelling anyone either."

"Was Lizzie there the entire time? Did she ever leave?"

"Guys," Scott says, "as much as I'd love to have a sit-down session to figure out how in purgatory's name there are so many werewolves, we need to figure out a plan of attack or an exit strategy because—wait . . . is that Kensey?" His jaw slackens as he stares at my nemesis and his occasional hookup.

"She's a vessel for a Fomorian witch. I warned you she was a back-stabbing, hex-throwing witch, only now you can see it for yourself."

He shivers at the potential ramifications. "Well, whatever she is, she's cooking up some type of curse that will be nasty."

All our attention shifts to Kensey. Her lips move as she palms dark smoke in her hands.

"Carman's not the only one familiar with Maleficium."

Witch Kensey smiles at me from across the flames. I can just imagine her saying, 'I am going to enjoy this." There are an exceptionally scary number of similarities between her and Carman—that's probably what attracted Breas to Kensey in the first place. Evil attracts evil.

"What should we do?" Scott says, shifting from foot to foot. "I'm not too keen on discovering how well Moralltach blocks curses."

"You named your sword?" Boys with their toys.

"Swords of honor all have names. Mine is Freagarach," Caer growls, her Fae canines flashing. "I say let's fight."

The last time Scott and I fought a crazed Maleficium witch, Dad and Calliope died in the crossfire. Tonight, we've already lost Gallean and Clarissa. I can't bear for anyone else to lose their life or risk injury. Caer might be ready to battle, but I'm not. Scott isn't either.

The shield bulges toward us as Witch Kensey starts pushing against it with her magical Maleficium smoke ball.

"The protections are breaking, Gigi," Scott says. "We have to get out of here. A portal would be great right about now."

Anna, Sam, Granda, and the rest of the coven nervously pace around the perimeter, chanting spells to keep the shields up.

I've only portal traveled with Scott.

"There are too many of us, and I won't leave them behind."

"No, there aren't. Join hands, everyone," Caer shouts.

The three of us take hands, further amplifying the power of the trí cumhacht. Alaric takes my other hand, Maddie takes his, and the rest of the coven members quickly form a large circle.

"Together," the three of us shout, and a giant portal pulls us through.

"No!" Witch Kensey and Breas roar, but the sound grows more and more distant as the portal removes us from the danger.

Portal hopping causes nasty side effects, especially when it's your first time, and when you're entirely human. The motion sickness can cause severe vomiting and dizziness—similar to riding a tilt-a-whirl by yourself five times in a row (and I speak from experience). Half the coven members collapse to their knees in exhaustion, clutching their stomachs. The other half crawl away on all fours, searching for some privacy so they can puke their brains out.

Anna recovers much faster than the others. She's portal jumped with Clarissa a few times. "Alysha? Bev? Are you okay?" she asks.

Alysha and Bev moan to indicate they're alive, but they still aren't sure how or why they feel so queasy.

"Milia, Chanti, where are you?" Sam, who also has some experience portal hopping with Granda and Clarissa, calls out.

"Over here," they sigh with considerable effort between dry heaves.

"Granda, Granda!" Scott shouts as he rushes over to his collapsed frame.

That's when everything goes to chaos in a handbasket.

Two werewolves launch themselves into the remains of our portal circle. Their teeth drip with saliva as loud growls fill the space. The smaller one is a cute-but-fearsome tan and white wolf. Lizzie. Her red eyes meet mine one second. The next, her muscles bunch and she launches herself at me. Her claws dig into my chest, sending me tumbling backward. Sharp canines snap at my exposed throat.

"No," Alaric roars.

Seconds before her teeth graze my skin, he rips her off of me and throws her across the circle. She spins around and growls, crouching down to relaunch herself at me.

"I said, no," Alaric's baritone voice rumbles, vibrating through the circle.

She hesitates.

"You will bow to me," he says. His tone leaves no room for argument. She crouches low as the alpha overpowers her.

Ferocious snarls tear my attention away from Lizzie. Granda's wrestling a large gray wolf with sadly familiar yellow eyes. Ryan. His teeth snap at Granda's chest. Scott raises his sword.

"No," I scream.

He pauses.

"Scott, don't kill him. It's Ryan."

Scott stumbles backward as if struck. "What?"

"It's Ryan and Lizzie." I point to Lizzie's now-folded frame bowing in front of Alaric. Her eyes flash red as she tries to fight his alpha command. She may also be the daughter of Clayone, but she ranks lower than her brother.

Granda screams and our attention immediately shifts back to where Ryan has him pinned against the ground. Caer catapults herself on top of Ryan and tears him off Granda. Scott drops his sword in surprise, dumbfounded at both Caer's raw power and the fact that the werewolf is his best friend who was supposed to be dead. Scott had pulled the trigger himself.

"Help her," I yell at him.

He snaps out of his daze and rushes to her aid. The two wrestle Ryan to the ground with brute force. His teeth snap at them as his four clawed paws try to push them off. He's a powerful werewolf, but they're far more powerful—especially together. They soon subdue him.

Lizzie emits a low growl as she continues to fight Alaric's dominance. Maddie stands beside her to ensure her obedience. He fingers the crystal around his neck, thankful that it keeps him from shifting into a wolf and turning on us. I've got a whole bowl of nightlock-imbued crystals inside. I'll force them on Lizzie and Ryan.

"Someone help us," Anna yells. She's trying to staunch the blood flowing from a wound on Granda's arm while Sam holds his blood-covered hands to Granda's carotid artery. "We're losing him!"

I can't lose him too. I can't. I head toward Granda's collapsed frame. There must be something I can do.

The Chalice of Healing, Brigit reminds me.

I can save them all. I lunge toward the front door.

"Gigi, we need your help now," Anna screams.

Her pleading freezes me in place. I war with myself. Take the time to get the chalice and the crystals, or try to heal him without it?

Alaric grunts as Lizzie launches herself at him, knocking him over. Her teeth snap at his chest. His crystal necklace— she's trying to tear it off of him and cause him to turn. How does she know the crystal is preventing him from turning?

"The crystals," Maddie yells, snapping me out of my daze. "Hurry."

Anna releases a string of curses, thinking I've abandoned them. I run into the house and grab the Chalice of Healing along with the bowl of crystals and sprint back outside.

"Here." I throw a crystal necklace at Maddie. He plucks it out of the air with his fast reflexes and prowls toward Lizzie, intent on circling it around her neck and turning her back into a girl.

"Scott, think fast," I shout and launch another one at him.

He releases Ryan with one hand and catches it on his middle finger. "Hold him," he yells to Caer—as if she needs a lesson on werewolf containment. From what I've seen, she's mastered that job.

Since I'm not as fast as Oegden, I slide across the ground to Granda on my knees. I've seen it done in movies a dozen times, so I figured if a plain old human can do it, why can't I? Granda's eyes widen as he sees what I'm cradling in my hands.

No, he wails in my mind, unable to speak aloud.

"Yes, and there's nothing you can do about it," I snap at

him, leaving no room for discussion in my voice as I slice my palm and start to chant.

To keep reading, grab your copy today...
Oak Moon: The Goddess Chronicles Book 5

Keep Reading for an excerpt for Throne of Silver, Silver Fae Book 1

THRONE OF SILVER: SILVER FAE BOOK ONE

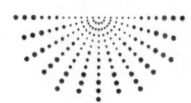

CHAPTER ONE

*D*ive in.

That was the advice the swim team captain gave me when I gingerly dipped my toe in the pool at my first 5:30 a.m. swim practice three years ago. You see, the cold shocks your body into action. Stroke after stroke, you concentrate on your breathing, and the angle of your arms as they reach and pull through the water, and the height and depth of your kick, rather than on the freezing temperatures —at least that's the idea anyway.

Dive in.

I took that advice to heart. Made it my life's mantra, really.

So, when Sami texted me about a summer fellowship at Trevnor University's Leadership Academy, I begged her to pick me up an application. I couldn't think of a better way to spend June, July, and August than adding Summer Fellowship to my Georgetown application. My early acceptance was all but guaranteed.

But the entrance exam was tomorrow, at the tail end of

my post-season training for States, and in the midst of planning prom, Spring Fling, and our junior class trip, plus track started Monday.

Dive in.

My mantra sometimes got me in over my head.

CHAPTER TWO

*L*aughter exploded around me as I hurried through the school's front entrance. Over by the water fountain, four seniors played Hacky Sack while an audience of giggly underclassmen watched, making noises accentuated with rounded oohs and angled aahs. They all probably went to last night's basketball game too—the lucky bastards. While I discussed table linens and canapés with hotel managers, they got to watch the Webster Titans trounce the Bay Cardinals, 90-40.

Sometimes I hated these classmates of mine.

I mean *really* hated them.

None of them had two hours of swim practice this morning. None of them had two meetings during school, another meeting after school, followed by two more hours of swim practice. None of them had a To Do list so complicated and involved, even I knew it wouldn't be completed until after graduation.

Sometimes I wondered what it would be like not to worry about tomorrow, or next week, or next year. To live in the moment and just *be*.

A long stream of water hit me square on the nose.

Or not...

Shocked gasps ping-ponged through the ten-foot wide, locker-lined hallway, followed by an awkward, collective silence.

My body flickered—it had been doing that a lot lately especially when I got mad or annoyed about something. It felt like ocean waves slamming against my chest, and no matter how strong a swimmer I was, sometimes the big ones knocked me on my ass even when I was only knee deep.

I took a few deep breaths to calm myself. Thankfully, the flickering stopped. I was never standing in front of a mirror when it happened so I didn't know if the flickering was something other people saw or it was just in my head— which concerned me on a number of levels, but I couldn't worry about any of that right now. Someone needed to be punished for their crime.

I tracked the gaze of the surprised onlookers. My assailant, an underclassman with an unsteady grip on a green squirt gun, shook in his red Nike sneakers. I wiped my face and flicked the water in his direction. The droplets soared through the air and landed on his flushed, round cheeks. To his credit, he took it like a man, but unfortunately for him, he became the target of the dark, foul mood that descended upon me the moment I stepped into school.

"Don't you have a place you need to be?"

"Y...yes, sssorry Starrrr," he said, adding an overflowing consonant stream in the already crowded hallway. I narrowed my eyes. He tossed the squirt gun into the garbage can and sprinted away, red Nikes and all. When the plastic toy landed at the bottom of the can, it was as if someone hit play and all the students returned to their regularly non-scheduled lives.

Yep, today, I *definitely* hated them.

I stomped through the crowds, throwing the occasional elbow and the well-directed shove, because evidently, I was still the only one who needed to be somewhere.

Frank's buzzed head towered over the sea of students. I caught a glimpse of tight red ringlets by his side and understood why he didn't wait for me after practice.

He glanced down the crowded hall. A broad smile crossed his face the moment he saw me. One icy vein thawed. "Hey Starr," he said, then winked at the redhead. "I'll see *you* later."

"Bye Frankie," she replied, smiling like she just won the boyfriend sweepstakes. Frank was the total package—tall, dark, handsome with the brains and personality to match, but he wouldn't date Little Red long enough for her to find out. He went through girls faster than he swam the fifty, and he held the school record in that.

I frowned at him. "Frankie?"

He shrugged.

I spun my combination into my locker. "She already has a nickname for you?"

He smirked.

I tried my combo again, but my locker refused to cooperate. It was like it wanted to add further insult to injury.

At least in this case, I could cause bodily harm to it without being frowned upon. I kicked the base of the locker since my foul mood hadn't completely lifted and kicking metal seemed like a productive means to releasing frustration. Plus I didn't know what was up with the whole body flickering thing. I wasn't even sure if I wanted to mention it to my best friend.

Frank rested his hands on my shoulders and guided me to the side. He hit the locker just below the locking mechanism, and it popped open. He smiled as he rested against the locker next to mine. "When you got it, you got it."

I rolled my eyes.

"You know, I'm considered quite a prince to every girl in this school but…" He zeroed in a finger on my nose.

I swatted it away. "I know how charming you can be. The entire female population of Roger G. Webster High knows how charming you can be."

He closed the distance between us. "I can't help it if girls find me irresistible, but my dating days would come to an end if you went out with me."

Most girls would love the attention Frank gave me. *Most* girls would grow red-faced and faint if they heard half the come-ons he practiced on me. *Most* girls haven't been best friends with him since he was a short, obnoxious, hormone-ridden, scrawny seventh grader who wore ratty yellow Sponge Bob t-shirts and couldn't get a date to save his life.

I shoved him into class. "Get a grip."

To keep reading, grab your copy of Throne of Silver: Silver Fae Book One

www.ingramcontent.com/pod-product-compliance
Lightning Source LLC
Chambersburg PA
CBHW020109180626
46812CB00006B/2530